Nursing a

GRUDGE

Nursing a
GRUDGE

Chris Well

BARBOUR
PUBLISHING

For my mother—hope it was worth the wait!

Cover design: Faceout Studio, www.faceoutstudio.com

Published by Barbour Publishing, Inc., P.O. Box 719, Uhrichsville, Ohio 44683, www.barbourbooks.com

Our mission is to publish and distribute inspirational products offering exceptional value and biblical encouragement to the masses.

 Member of the
Evangelical Christian
Publishers Association

Printed in the United States of America.

Cast of Characters

Earl Walker has given up: on God, on the world, on himself. A resident of Candlewick Retirement Community in Mt. Hermit, Kentucky, Earl hasn't left his wheelchair since a bullet put an end to his career as a bus driver. In the years following the death of his beloved wife, Barbara, Earl has been alone. And he prefers it that way.

College student **Jenny Hutton** is determined to bring Earl out of his shell. A member of New Love Fellowship Church, Jenny sees it as her spiritual duty to reach out and help the old man see his need for God and the world.

The Victim and the Suspects

Dandy Anderson has a gambling problem. How desperate was he to get out of debt?

Sally Brouwer has a little problem with stealing. How far would she go to keep it quiet?

Mark Conroy has a history with the victim that goes back some sixty years. Did they share some horrible secret?

George Kent was a bully who didn't care who he pushed around. But he must have pushed somebody too far. . . .

Gloria Logan was always fighting off unwanted advances from the victim. Just how badly did she want to be left alone?

Ed Nelson, managing director of Candlewick, is scrambling to engineer a cover-up. But to avoid publicity—or for some darker reason?

Ray Stanton was bullied for years. What was he willing to do to make it stop?

CHAPTER ONE

Earl Walker twisted in his wheelchair and took his eyes off the small television screen long enough to point. "You missed a spot over there."

Feather duster in hand, Jenny Hutton wrinkled her nose. "You know, Mr. Walker, I didn't come here to dust. I'm not your maid." She stood there awkwardly.

Earl leaned forward in his chair, rubbing his hand over his closely cropped gray hair. "You told me that you wanted to be useful."

"No, I said I wanted *you* to be useful." She stopped, her eyes widening. "I mean, I'm here to help you be useful. That is, I. . ." She gave up, pushing her glasses up the bridge of her nose. "Um, where did you say that dust was?"

He pointed. "Over there."

Jenny resumed dusting. "This apartment is twice the size of my dorm room."

Earl's living arrangements at Candlewick Retirement Community included a living room, bedroom, kitchenette, half dining room, and bathroom.

Jenny made another attempt at conversation. "My name is

Jenny Hutton. *Jenny*. And I'll be visiting you here at Candlewick every Saturday." She scooted the small television on the dresser to the left and began moving dust around. "I'm a volunteer from my church."

She scooted the television back into place and looked at Earl again. He supposed his red flannel shirt clashed with the afghan across his knees, but he didn't bother with appearances—even for a young female visitor.

"And I appreciate it." Earl glanced over from his TV. "How about getting that behind the dresser?"

"Where?" Jenny squinted. "Oh—I didn't see that because I was standing over here." She glanced at his wheelchair, and her face turned red. "Oh! Wait! I didn't—" She went to a chair and sat. After a moment she spoke again in a soft voice. "Maybe we could just talk." She looked at his television show. "What are you watching there?"

He grunted. "It's pro wrestling. They have it on every Saturday."

Jenny watched the TV a few minutes. Then she glanced over at Earl, who quickly feigned riveted attention to the action onscreen. "How can you watch this stuff? You know it's all made up, right?"

"Of course. It's television." He pointed to the fracas on the screen. "Like this right here. The Annoyed Aztec and Joe 'Voodoo' Mortimer are having—well, let's just say—their differences."

"He hit the guy over the head with a chair."

"Like what I said: 'differences.' "

Wrinkling her brow, Jenny got up from the chair and went to the television. "Would you mind if we didn't watch this right now?" She shut off the set.

"Hey! Idol Hanz is going to be in the next match!"

"Please."

Earl's shoulders sagged. "Fine."

Jenny smiled and went to the curtains, tying them back. Light burst into the room. "There! That's better. You need sunshine— it's got vitamin D."

He grunted. "I don't know if I believe that."

"Of course it does. They did a study."

"Pfft. That what they teach you in college?"

"Um, no. Actually, I'm studying to be a counselor." Returning to the chair, Jenny looked at the collection of framed photographs on the coffee table. She grabbed one of them and picked it up for a closer look. "Is this you with your wife? She's pretty."

Earl smiled. "That's Barbara. We were married just a few years in that picture. We were so young then."

Jenny looked at the other frames on the table. "I don't see any pictures of kids."

"Barbara and I never had children." His voice cracked. "We thought we had all the time in the world."

Changing the subject quickly, she grabbed at a framed certificate. "What's this for?"

"That's a commendation. I was a metro bus driver for twenty-five years." Earl grunted. "It was right after that I got shot in the leg."

"I'm sorry." Her voice was so soft Earl could barely hear it.

"You didn't do it."

"I'm not apologizing. I'm sympathizing." Jenny placed the frame back. She latched onto a stapled document, which turned out to be the official newsletter of Candlewick Retirement Community. The headline across the top blared RESIDENTS GIVEN 30 DAYS. "What's this about?"

Earl shrugged. "A state inspector came around, and I guess

Candlewick failed inspection. They say residents have a month to find another place to live."

"What?" Jenny jerked upright. "It seems like such a nice place! How could it not be up to code?"

He shrugged again. "You'd have to take that up with the state."

"This issue is already a couple of weeks old—do you know where you're going yet?"

He studied the carpet. "I do not need a babysitter."

"I'm not trying to be your babysitter. I'm just a friend."

"I don't need one of those, either," Earl grumbled. He folded his hands on his lap, set his jaw, and gazed at her with stony eyes.

Jenny changed the subject again. "What do your friends here at Candlewick do?"

"I wouldn't call them friends."

"Okay then, your acquaintances."

"I wouldn't call them—"

"People. What do people here at Candlewick do?"

"We watch TV. In fact, *Wheel of Fortune* is on soon."

"Television is no substitute for real people." Jenny leaned forward and put a hand on his knee. "Mr. Walker. . ." At his sharp glare, she yanked her hand back. "Mr. Walker, we all need people. God made us that way."

"I don't know about that."

"Here, I'll show you." She went to her backpack by the door, dug through it, pulled out a leather-bound Bible, and returned to her chair. "Let's see." Adjusting her glasses, she thumbed through the first few pages. "Ah, here! 'It is not good for the man to be alone.' "

He snorted. "I'm flattered, but I don't want to marry you."

"I didn't mean *that*." Jenny blushed. "Sorry—I mean, I'm sure you're a very nice man. But I'm not ready to—um—" She bit her lip and looked down at her Bible again. "Let's see. . .oh! Here! 'Two are better than one, because they have a good return for their work: If one falls down, his friend can help him up.' " She looked up from her Bible and beamed at Earl. "That's in Ecclesiastes."

"Uh-huh, that's great. Look, if I let you wheel me on down to the recreation center, will you stop preaching at me?"

Jenny's face lit up. "The recreation center—that's perfect! So, I guess Candlewick residents do a lot of activities there?"

Earl's shoulders twitched. "Your guess is as good as mine."

"You've never been?"

"I got the tour when I moved in five years ago."

Jenny gasped. "Five years!" She got up and gripped the handles on the back of Earl's wheelchair. "Well, what are we waiting for?"

Outside the apartment, Jenny pushed the wheelchair to the end of the hall and through the glass door outside to the common garden area, a circular open area surrounded by the big Candlewick building. She stopped and breathed in the crisp air. "That smell is so sweet. What is that?"

"Honeysuckle. Barbara loved the stuff." His voice was wistful.

"It's so peaceful out here." Jenny looked at him. "Do you ever just come out here to contemplate God's beautiful creation?"

"I can contemplate from inside the apartment."

"But this garden is so beautiful."

"It could use some work over there." Earl pointed out some of the rough patches of weeds. He turned his attention back to the girl. "Now, to make sure we're on the same page, you wheel me down there for a few minutes, say hello to a few people, and you promise to get me back here in time for *Wheel of Fortune*. Right?"

"You'll get some fresh air, and you'll meet some people. It'll be great."

"That doesn't sound like a promise."

Without answering, Jenny gripped the handles on the back of the wheelchair and looked around to get her bearings. "Let's see, which way to the recreation center?"

"You promise to bring me back, right?" Earl's voice was shaky. "Right?"

"Fine." The young lady pushed the wheelchair toward the glass doors back into the main building. "Now, which way do we go? This place is like a maze."

Earl pointed down one hall, and they ended up at the Candlewick library. It was a warm and inviting medium-sized room, with worn but comfortable chairs surrounding a big reading table. The shelves were chock-full of books. A selection of magazines lined one wall.

Jenny wanted to ask for directions, but Earl was adamant. "We can find it ourselves."

"But if you don't know where it is. . ."

He pointed down another hall. "Just go that way."

At the chapel, they were too late for the Saturday morning service and too early for the Saturday evening service. During these middle hours the chapel was open for anyone who wanted to pray or meditate. Visitors had their choice of rickety wooden chairs.

"Nobody here," Earl grumped. He pointed down a third hall. "That way."

Down another hall, they reached a dead end that was the Candlewick general store. It was a small room with faded paneling along the walls.

"I really thought we had it this time," Earl said.

"Well, I'm asking for directions."

"Suit yourself." Earl tapped his watchless wrist. "Just remember, we're on a schedule."

Despite the room's small size, it still seemed to hit all the necessary highlights—from paper goods, greeting cards, and pre-packaged foods to clothing and toiletries. There were two men at the counter, talking. Jenny stepped around the customer and got the attention of the man behind the counter, who gave her a friendly smile. "Yes ma'am, how may I help you today?"

She pushed her glasses up on her nose. "Hello! We're trying to find the recreation center. Can you give us directions?"

Taking a deep breath, the man scratched the back of his head. "Oh sure. Just go out this door, and hang a left—"

"No Clem," the shopper butted in, setting his canned goods on the counter. "They want to head to the right."

"I'm telling this, Alfred."

"But you're telling it wrong."

The clerk shook his head emphatically. "No I'm not. You go out that exit there and take a left. . . ."

"Oh," the shopper countered, "you mean that door over there. I thought you were sending them out this door over here. That's different."

"I know that."

"But they can get there faster without—"

"But it's so much easier if you just go straight through—"

Trying to follow the directions, Earl and Jenny got turned around and ended up at the computer room. Inside, two long tables were set up with privacy partitions every few feet. Each workspace offered a computer monitor, keyboard, and mouse. Muted light from curtained windows aided the bright florescent lights. The stations were manned by Candlewick residents browsing the Internet, checking their e-mail, and updating spreadsheets.

A rich male voice from behind them asked, "May I help you folks?" Earl turned to see a young man in a striped blue shirt and tan pants.

Jenny blushed. "Yes, please, um. . ." She glanced at his nametag quickly. "Grant Caine." She curled strands of blond hair behind her ear. "I'm Jenny. We're trying to find the recreation center."

"Hello, Jenny." The young man grinned broadly at Earl. "So, is this your grandfather?"

"We're not related." Earl fidgeted. "Can we just get the directions and be done with it?"

Jenny made an apologetic face. "This is Earl Walker. He's, um, on a schedule."

Caine spoke with calm understanding. "Don't be embarrassed, sir. A lot of our residents here have certain, um, *medical* conditions that make them have to rush home."

Earl was mortified at the suggestion. "I've got a TV show to watch, young man!"

Jenny repeated the apologetic face. "He just wants to stop in at the recreation center first."

"And he's having trouble remembering his way around?"

"I never knew my way around!"

"Here, I'll print you a map of the complex." Caine went to one of the nearest computers. He clicked open a document and soon had the floor plan of Candlewick Retirement Community. "Here's a map of the whole place." *Click, click.* He pointed to the machine against the wall. "It should come out there in a second."

"Thanks." Jenny smiled, twirling strands of her hair again. "This is a great computer room."

"All the equipment was donated. Not top-of-the-line, I'm afraid, but they do the job."

"So. . .does everyone have access here?"

"Sure. Mr. Walker can check his e-mail, go online, design his own personal stationery—the works." Caine led her across the room to the printer. "And this also works as a copy machine."

"So, people can just—"

"Wait." Caine squinted at the printer's digital screen. He pressed a few buttons, but nothing happened. "Weird. It was working this morning."

"Don't worry about the map," Jenny said. "We'll find it."

"Hey, I know." Caine looked at her, flashing pearly whites. "I'll show you to the recreation room myself."

Jenny's eyes lit up. "Would you?"

"Yes," Earl gushed in mock glee, "would you?" As Earl wheeled down the hall, he saw the young man and Jenny trade several amused glances.

Finally the boy led them to a large carpeted room. "Here we go, the recreation center." Caine bent to offer Earl his hand. "It was good meeting you, sir. I hope you have a great evening."

Earl grimaced and kept his hands to himself. "Same to you."

Caine flashed another grin at Jenny. "Hope to see you again soon."

She blushed. "Me, too." Jenny watched him walk away.

Earl cleared his throat and tapped his wrist again. "Tick-tock."

"Oh! Yes sir."

"Now, remember—just a few minutes, and we go back for *Wheel*, right?"

"Don't be such a grump." Jenny squeezed his shoulder. "What's the worst that could happen?"

CHAPTER ⚏ TWO

The recreation center was enormous—Earl stopped for a moment to take it all in. Light burst in through huge windows, casting shadows across the dark red carpet. Those residents not relaxing in comfy chairs chatting or watching television were engaged in one of several activities, from darts to cards to billiards to board games.

In front of a huge TV, a group of people erupted into cheers. Earl frowned. "What is going on over there?"

Jenny laughed. "It looks they're. . .bowling."

A woman with big red hair stood up. Holding some sort of control device, she went through the motions of bowling. On the TV, a digital bowling ball rolled up the pixel aisle with a synthetic rumble. It hit the virtual bowling pins and all ten fell. Everyone in her group cheered, throwing their hands in the air. The woman took a bow, handed the device to the next player, and went to her chair.

Jenny wheeled Earl over to the table. "Can we watch?"

The woman smiled and waved them over. "The more the merrier. I'm Gloria."

"Hi, I'm Jenny."

Gloria's eyes twinkled at Earl. "And who's your friend?"

"This is Earl Walker." Jenny whispered loudly, "He doesn't have any friends here at Candlewick."

"Hello." Gloria smiled. "Has anyone told you that you have the most amazing blue eyes?"

Earl fidgeted. Was he blushing? "Hello."

Gloria nodded toward her friends around the table, who were intent on the bowling game. "Hey, gang—this is Earl and Jenny." The others waved and said hello as Gloria pointed them out. "That's Ray Stanton. . .Mark Conroy. . .Sally Brouwer. . .and Dandy Anderson." The last one, standing against the wall, did a little dance shuffle, ending with a salute.

Jenny wheeled Earl closer to the table. "I'm surprised to find y'all bowling."

"It's very popular around here," Sally said. She nodded, her long black hair bobbing up and down. "This is the big bowling tournament. We're sending our results on to the regional committee."

Anderson put a hand on Conroy's shoulder. "Come on, ten bucks. Just ten bucks."

The other man shook his head. "I'm not betting you ten bucks."

Gloria told Earl in a low voice, "Dandy takes medicine for his legs. One of the side effects is that it makes him gamble."

Earl nodded uncertainly. He had no idea how to answer something like that.

The game continued for several minutes. When Gloria's turn came up again, she turned to Earl. "Hey, Blue Eyes, do you bowl?"

He shook his head emphatically. "No."

"C'mon," she said. "You can have my turn. You don't even have to leave your chair."

"I'd rather not."

Gloria hesitated then shrugged. "Suit yourself."

As she went, Jenny murmured into Earl's ear, "I like her."

He grumbled back, "Then you can stay here with her while I go back to my TV. I'll just bet that Pat Sajack is about to—"

He was cut off by a ruckus across the room. At the billiards table, a big man with wavy gray hair and dark glasses pushed someone aside. Jenny asked, "What's going on over there?"

"That would be George Kent." Sally made a sour face. "He considers himself the big man at Candlewick."

Over at the billiards table, Kent grabbed a ball and shoved it into the others, ruining the game in progress. He let out an obnoxious guffaw and walked away. The others at the table simply started collecting the balls to start over.

Around the room, everyone stopped what they were doing. As Kent strode across the carpet, all eyes were on him. Once it was clear that the man was headed for the bowling group, the other activities slowly picked back up.

"Great," Stanton muttered. "He's coming here."

"Just tell him to go away," Sally said.

"You try telling him!"

Kent howled a greeting, and the group around the table gave a half-hearted reply. Kent glanced at the screen. "What'cha got here? Bowling? Let me try."

Sally shouted, "We're in the middle of the tournament!"

"C'mon. Stanton don't mind." He turned to Ray Stanton. "Do you?"

The other man hesitated then handed over the controller. "I guess not."

Jenny rustled as if she were about to say something. Earl put a hand on her arm and shook his head.

Standing in front of the screen, Kent analyzed the device. "How does this work?"

"Well, um, you see. . . ." Stanton trembled. "You swing it like this. And the machine knows when you're bowling."

"What'll they think of next?" Kent turned toward the table, taking off his ring. Earl noticed the big white stone as the man held it out for Conroy to see. "Take a look at that, man. It's huge!" He then held it out for Gloria. "Would you watch this for me, doll?"

"Just set it on the table," Gloria said. "And my name is Mrs. Logan."

Kent laughed and winked. As he set the ring on the table, he looked at Sally Brouwer and frowned. Then he suddenly regarded Dandy Anderson. "Hey—wanna make it interesting?"

Everyone looked at Dandy. The man's eyes grew wide. "What did you have in mind?"

"I don't know. . . ." Kent seemed to consider it. "Double or nothing?"

Jenny leaned for Earl's ear. "Double or nothing of what?" Earl didn't answer; he merely watched the others exchange nervous glances.

Licking his lips, Anderson asked, "What's the bet?"

A predatory grin spread across Kent's face. "That I bowl a strike."

Anderson gave it some thought. Everyone waited. Finally he started nodding—slowly at first—then picking up steam until his whole body was in it. "Sure. Sure."

"All right." Kent, pleased, turned to the screen. He got into place just so, flexed his fingers around the control, and went for it. The digital ball shot down the digital lane and smacked in the center of the digital pins. A strike. Kent howled.

Jenny looked at Mr. Anderson. All the blood had drained from his face.

Kent glanced at Stanton. "Now, that wasn't so bad, was it?" Stanton wore an embarrassed smile but said nothing. Kent turned to Anderson again. "So, do you wanna let it ride?"

Gloria put a hand on Anderson's arm. "Don't."

The man shook his head slowly. "I. . .I can't."

"Suit yourself." Kent lined up and let the virtual ball fly. On-screen it scooted for the gutter. Kent cursed and slammed the controller down on the table then looked at Anderson and laughed. "You should'a taken the bet." The other man, his face red, didn't reply. Kent turned his attention to Gloria. "Say, doll, what say you and me—"

She cut him off, scowling. "What say you just go and leave me out of it?"

Kent laughed. "You don't know what you're missing." Snatching his ring off the table, he held it up for Mark Conroy to see. "How about that stone, huh? Finding one that big is harder than you'd think." Conroy didn't reply. Kent added, "So, is the party still on?"

"Sure thing," Conroy said, barely making eye contact. He forced a weak grin.

After the big man exited, Gloria pointed at the TV. "What about Dandy's score? Will this thing let him have a do over?"

Anderson stood up, shaking his head. He was the image of a broken man. "Don't worry about it. I'm done."

Everyone at the table exchanged pained looks. It looked to Earl like a dark cloud had settled over the table.

"Come on," Conroy said, trying to rally them. "We can't let him spoil it for us. Let's go eat." Slowly the group agreed, everyone getting up to go.

Gloria touched Earl on the knee. "Hey, we're having a get-together. Wanna come along?"

Conroy shot her a look.

Earl coughed into his hand. "Actually, we have to get back. We have plans."

Jenny said loudly, "Oh Mr. Walker, you can watch TV any night of the week." She smiled at Gloria. "We'd love to, thanks."

When Gloria went for her purse, Earl grumbled at Jenny. "What do you think you're doing?"

"Come on, it'll be fun." She winked. "What's the worst that could happen?"

Feeling like a helpless captive, Earl felt he had no choice but to go along with the college girl and the lady bowler. While Jenny and Gloria chatted, he took note of his surroundings in case he got a chance to make a break for it later.

Occasionally shooting a nervous glance in Earl's direction, Mark Conroy led the way down the hall toward the residential section. On the way to his apartment, various Candlewick residents stopped him in the hall to discuss the party in hushed tones. Earl had to wonder what the big deal was.

The entourage passed George Kent in the hall. He was standing in an apartment doorway, hand on the knob, arguing with a younger man. Earl recognized the second man, having seen his face in the newsletter—he was Ed Nelson, managing director for Candlewick Retirement Community. Just before they were out of sight, Earl thought he saw Nelson handing something to Kent.

Earl looked up at Gloria and Jenny, who were both still chatting away. They hadn't noticed a thing.

Pfft. Women.

At Conroy's apartment, their host gave crashers Jenny and Earl a look but still exuded politeness. "Welcome, friends, come in." Conroy leaned over and said to Earl, "I hope you appreciate that this is something of a secret."

Earl raised an eyebrow. "That so?"

"Ray's special chili has been in the slow cooker a few hours." He checked his watch. "Should be ready soon."

"And you don't want the neighbors to know?"

"It's the nurses I'm worried about."

"Chili is off a lot of our diets," Gloria chimed in. "Not to mention every time Ray makes chili, he makes it hotter and hotter."

Conroy looked at Jenny. "So don't tell the nurses, right?"

Gloria patted the man on the arm. "Don't worry, Mark, they won't spoil your good time." Leaving Conroy at the door to greet other guests, Gloria helped Jenny maneuver Earl's chair through the apartment, around partygoers and furniture. Earl situated himself in a far corner, between the couch and the wall. The ladies each took a seat on the couch.

The folks in the room chatted in hushed tones. Every few minutes there was a special knock at the door. Conroy would check the peephole then open up and greet the newcomers. Several of them came by the couch and spoke with Gloria, who in turn introduced them to Earl and Jenny.

When the party seemed in full swing, Gloria stood. "I need to check on Ray in the kitchen." She winked at Earl. "I'll be right back, Blue Eyes." He didn't answer.

After Gloria was out of earshot, Jenny leaned over. She said in a low but thrilled voice, "Mr. Walker, she is totally into you."

"You're crazy."

"No, I'm not." Jenny waved around at the socializing going on around them. "And see, Mr. Walker? All these people are your age. It must be great for you."

Earl looked for a clock. Wondering whether *Wheel of Fortune* was on, he thumbed toward the TV across the room. "Does that work?"

"Come on, Mr. Walker, it's not that bad, is it?"

"No. It's worse."

There was another secret knock, and Conroy let in another batch of new wrinkled faces. Gloria reappeared and introduced Jenny around.

Earl kept to himself. Bored, his eyes took in the party. Across the room, Dandy Anderson was demonstrating some sort of soft-shoe routine. Sally Brouwer and Ray Stanton were in and out of the kitchen, Stanton's loud, flower-patterned Hawaiian shirt apparently signifying his readiness to "party." Gloria and Jenny were busy chatting with some others.

Conroy, at the door, got Sally's attention. "Could you get the beverages started? I still have to watch the door."

Sally Brouwer disappeared into the kitchen. She returned in a few minutes with a tray of glasses. Eventually she came around to Jenny. "Would you like a drink?"

"Sally, wait!" It was Conroy, yelling from the front door. "Chili first, then the drinks!"

"Oh. Okay."

There was a commotion at the door. George Kent had arrived, his ego quickly filling the room. "You call this a party? Why is everyone so quiet?"

Conroy tried to control the situation. "We don't want the staff to find out about this. So if you could just keep your voice down, so we don't—"

"No problem," he bellowed. "I'll save your party." Kent slapped the host hard on the back. Then seeing Jenny and Gloria on the couch, he came over. He was carrying some sort of box—the one Earl saw the manager give him in the hall—which he threw on the coffee table. Kent plopped down on the couch next to the ladies, who scooted over to give him space. Chomping gum loudly, he reached out and clutched Gloria's knee. "Miss me much, babe?" He tried to nuzzle her ear.

"Get off me!" Gloria pushed him away. "I've told you a hundred times to—"

"Oh, you know you like a forceful man. Women who protest are just playing hard to get." Kent turned and winked at Earl, laughing. "Ain't that right?"

Earl squirmed but didn't answer. Gloria plucked Kent's hand off her knee.

He simply turned his attention to Jenny, putting his arm around her. "You're new to these shindigs. Who might you be?"

Earl jumped in. "A girl young enough to be your granddaughter."

Kent looked at him uncertainly then leaned back and let out a hearty laugh, ending with that howl. Earl looked over toward the kitchen and saw Ray Stanton peek out and pop back in.

Kent stood up. "Excuse me a second, ladies." He wound his way around the party guests and into the kitchen.

Jenny said to Gloria, "Everyone at Candlewick seems to be having so much fun."

The older woman giggled. "Sometimes it's like camp."

Jenny was going to say something else, when there was some shouting from the kitchen. Judging by their raised voices, Kent and Stanton had gotten into some kind of fracas, followed by a clatter of metal objects bouncing on the linoleum floor.

Conroy, still at the door, started for the kitchen but stopped abruptly. Others around the room hushed, trading glances. In a couple seconds, Kent came out, tucking some bills in his pocket. He noticed everyone looking at him and laughed, plopping back on the couch.

"Sally," Conroy said, "maybe you could tell the gang in the kitchen to start serving the chili?"

"Sure." Sally, joined by Gloria and Dandy, went into the kitchen. In a few minutes she started bringing the bowls out. Kent started yelling for his, so Sally hurried to serve him, if only (Earl assumed) to shut him up.

She then offered bowls to Earl and Jenny. "Try some! It's delicious."

Conroy appeared suddenly. "Actually, I don't think there's enough to go around." He looked at Earl. "I hope you understand."

"Fine with me," Earl said.

Jenny smiled at Sally. "Thanks anyway."

As steaming bowls of chili were served around the room, the chatter dwindled—everyone eating, popping acid reflux pills, or working their inhalers. The silence didn't last for long. Kent demanded another helping of chili. "More!" he howled. "More!" He banged his spoon against his bowl. Finally Sally took his bowl into the kitchen and brought out seconds.

After his third bowl, Kent grabbed the box he had brought and opened it to reveal cigars. He held one out. "Take a look. Cubans."

Earl waved them off. "I don't smoke."

"I wasn't offering." Kent chewed off the end of the cigar. When he couldn't find an ashtray, he spit it into someone's unattended glass. Then he yelled for their host. "Conroy! Got a light?"

Conroy, still tied up by the door, yelled toward the kitchen. "Dandy!" When he saw the hoofer pop out, Conroy said, "Get some matches out of the drawer there for Kent."

Anderson got the box of matches and sheepishly brought it over. He tried to open the box, but his hands were trembling. Finally, the man gave up and tossed the whole box over to Kent and walked away briskly.

Kent laughed. He got out a wooden match then carelessly tossed the open box onto the coffee table, where the matches dumped out. Jenny jumped up to clean the mess.

Puffing away on his cigar, Kent propped his feet up on the table. "Hey, girl, get a load of this." He took off his ring and held it out to Jenny. "Look at the size of that stone."

Gloria returned to Earl and Jenny. "Sorry I've been gone. I was helping Ray put together an ice pack."

Earl raised an eyebrow. "I don't suppose it was a cooking-related injury?"

Gloria glanced darkly at Kent and back. "No."

Sally came around with a tray of drinks. Jenny looked at the tray doubtfully. "Um, what is it?"

"Rum," Sally leaned in and whispered. "Don't tell the nurses."

Jenny smiled weakly. "I don't want to be impolite, but I don't drink."

Earl nodded toward her. "She's a church girl."

Sally flinched. "Oh. I'm sorry." She turned to Earl. "I don't guess. . . ?"

Earl smiled and shook his head. "Thank you, no."

Sally turned to Kent. "Drink?" When she noticed the ring, she couldn't take her eyes off it.

"Now, you know I don't drink since the kidney transplant."

Kent put the ring on the coffee table, took a puff of his cigar, and blew the smoke right at her. "Besides, I don't even have a glass."

"Gloria," Conroy said, "there's some juice in the fridge. Could you get some for George?"

As she got up, Gloria said to Jenny and Earl, "There's milk, if you want. That's what I'm having."

Earl grunted. "Milk's fine."

Gloria returned with a glass of grape juice for Kent—he winked, but she ignored it—and three glasses of milk, one each for Jenny, Earl, and herself. Conroy appeared again in the center of the room. "A toast!" He held his glass of rum high, the others doing likewise. Kent held up his grape juice. Jenny and Gloria held up their milk. Earl abstained. Conroy, eyes taking in the hushed group, said, "To health, to life, to love." Everyone drank to that.

George Kent drank down to the bottom of his purple beverage and smacked his lips. He took a couple more puffs on his cigar. It looked to Earl like the man's eyes were glazing over. He might not have been drinking alcohol, but he looked to Earl like the drunkest man in the place. "That's really something. You know, I think—" He stopped speaking suddenly. He stood and swayed, clutching his side. His face grew red. He looked nauseous.

Kent stumbled and fell by Earl's feet. Then he gagged and tried to claw his way up Earl's legs. Earl was frightened the man might get sick on him if they didn't get Kent off him quick.

Conroy pointed to Stanton, standing over by the kitchen. "Hey Ray, could you and Dandy help Kent back home?"

The two men took each side of Kent and helped him up. As they reached the door, Kent began to gag again, flailing. The men lost their grip. Kent yelled with pain and, banging his head on the door frame, hit the hard floor.

Earl glared at Jenny. "*This* is the worst that could happen."

CHAPTER ⚏ THREE

Earl barely slept that night. Images kept flickering through his mind—of the party, of Kent collapsing like that, of how everyone behaved afterward.

After Kent hit the floor, the other two men finally got him back up and headed down the hall, presumably to get the sick man home to his apartment. Meanwhile, the party petered out. Conroy busied himself inspecting the coffee table and couch around where Kent had sat. Gloria and Sally had gathered up the glasses, bowls, and silverware. Then Sally came and started examining the carpet around Earl's wheelchair.

Gloria and Stanton came out of the kitchen, the man sporting something of a shiner. Stanton stopped by the coffee table and took a peek out of his one good eye. But the strain seemed too much, and he needed Gloria to help guide him to the door. On the way out she said her apologies to Earl and Jenny.

The party officially over, Earl and Jenny had followed the rest out. He hadn't said much to the college girl after that, and in retrospect he felt like maybe he should have said something. Deep down he knew he was being far too grumpy to such a nice young girl. But somehow it came easy.

Of course, what kept him awake were thoughts of a woman named Gloria. . . .

———

He took it slowly the next morning. In fact, he was still in his pajamas that afternoon when there was someone at the door.

It was Jenny. "May I come in?"

Earl regarded her a brief second then shrugged lightly. He put hands to his chair's wheels and rolled back from the door.

Jenny came in. "How are you doing? I suppose you heard about Mr. Kent."

"What happened?"

"He died in the night of kidney failure."

Earl pulled his chair back into a corner. "I'm not surprised."

"Bless your heart." Jenny found her way to a chair. "Is that a different blanket?"

Earl looked at the blanket across his knees, nodded, and then thumbed to the afghan thrown on the couch. "After he pawed all over it, drooling like that. . .well, I thought it'd be good to wash that before I use it again."

They sat in silence. Earl felt like he should try to entertain her somehow—after all, she came out all this way—but no useful ideas came to mind. Finally he said, "You seem to be dressed for something."

"Oh—yeah, I went to church this morning. Did you?" She looked at him and apparently realized a man in his pajamas probably had not. She continued. "After what happened yesterday, I had some trouble focusing on the service. You know, after I called the front desk about Mr. Kent and all."

"Uh-huh."

"I had hoped that the service would help take my mind off

things. But even after I got to church, my state of mind didn't improve by much. I mumbled through the hymns. I barely listened to the announcements. I just couldn't focus. All I could think about was that poor man, George Kent. I couldn't put out of my mind the look of pain on the man's face when he fell to the floor."

Earl tried to think of something to say. He said, "Uh-huh."

"And then as Pastor Benton went to the podium for the sermon, I had out my notebook and pen. I was determined to focus." She sighed. "But after some twenty minutes, the sermon was suddenly over and my notebook page was still blank."

"Would you like some. . .tea or something?"

"No, thank you." She smiled weakly. "After the service, I was able to talk with the pastor. Actually I started to bawl, standing right there in the church atrium."

Earl rubbed his hands nervously. "Is that so?"

Jenny nodded. "Then Pastor Benton took me to his office in the back of the church, where I shared with him the events of, well, you know. I may have cried some more."

His heart went out to someone so fragile. But he still didn't know what to do for her. Finally he asked, "So, what did he say?"

"That the Lord never gives us more than we can handle."

"Really?"

"He admitted that it sounds cliché but said that sometimes the cliché is true." She chuckled. "He also told me to step back and look at this in context."

"Context? What context?"

"Well, this wasn't something that happened while I was on, say, a ride along with the county sheriff. Or out with emergency workers."

"If you say so."

"I was at a small gathering and someone died of natural causes." Jenny hesitated. She took off her glasses and wiped them. "I'm not saying it wasn't horrible. But if it had happened at, say, the mall—would I be sitting here wondering if the Lord didn't want me to go back to the mall? I mean, where would I get my shoes then?"

"Hmm." Earl felt his patience was wavering. This was the longest conversation he'd had with any one person in years. "I see what you mean."

"I mean, I can't expect these people to just drop in front of me like that each time I come here, right?" She looked at Earl, her eyes widening. "I'm sorry, I didn't mean. . ."

Earl forced himself to smile. "Don't worry about it. Besides, if they keep having these wild parties. . ." He grunted. "I guess it's a wonder only one of them died."

Jenny gave a nervous laugh. "Okay, it was a pretty tame party by college standards." She stopped. "Not that I go to a lot of college parties."

"I understand."

"Of course, I never saw so many in one room using inhalers and taking antacids." She hesitated. "Mr. Walker, I know you must feel just awful about what happened yesterday. Seeing a man cut down like that in the prime of his life. I want you to know that it's okay to be sad. It's healthy to grieve."

Earl didn't know how to respond.

Jenny dug in her backpack for her Bible. "Here, Mr. Walker." She checked the pages in the back then turned to the middle. 'A sad face is good for the heart.' That's Ecclesiastes 7:3." She looked back up at him.

Nothing.

She tried again, flipping some pages. "Okay—from Proverbs: 'There is a way that seems right to a man. . . .' Oh, um." She flipped some more pages. Here. . . 'Cursed be the day I was born!' Wait, Jeremiah—Jeremiah? Ha!" She checked the back of the Bible again then flipped back to the middle. "'There is a time for everything, and a season for every activity under heaven: a time to be born and a time to die.'" She looked at him. "That's Ecclesiastes 3:1–2," she said. "There's a time for everything, Mr. Walker. There's good things; there's bad things. . . ."

Earl found himself staring somewhere else. Thinking.

Jenny barely spoke above a whisper. "Mr. Walker, I'm so sorry. If I hadn't taken you there, if I hadn't pressured you to go meet all those people. . ." Her voice cracked. "You just wanted to stay here and watch your TV shows. I'm sorry—I'm so sorry." She started to shudder.

He put a hand on her arm. "Stop your crying, College. I'm not disturbed because George Kent died."

"Y–you're not?"

"No. I'm disturbed because it was so convenient for him to die."

She sniffled. "Why would you say that?"

Hunched over in his wheelchair, Earl stared out through the crack in the curtain at the common garden outside. "Everyone in that room hated George Kent. Some of them may have pretended to like him; some of them may have tolerated him. But behind those grins was a lot of seething hatred."

"What are you saying? That Mr. Kent was. . .*murdered*?"

Earl stared at her a second, weighing his answer. Finally, he shrugged. "It's crossed my mind."

The girl wrinkled her nose. "Lots of people hate other people.

That doesn't make them murderers."

"Then there was our trip through the hall. Kent had some private conversation with the managing director, Ed Nelson, before the party."

"We all talked to people right before the party. None of us dropped dead afterward. That doesn't make them want to murder you."

"Aw, forget it." Earl rubbed his chin. "I just can't explain it."

"You should try to relax, Mr. Walker. You were pushed out of your comfort zone. Then something awful happened, and now you're trying to make sense of it. Sometimes people just have accidents."

"You call that an accident?"

"Well, some people get sick. Whatever." Jenny smiled weakly. "Sometimes people just drop dead. Especially when they're old." She glanced at Earl and turned red again. "Oh! I'm sorry. I didn't—"

"Of course you did." Earl grunted. "I am old. George Kent was old. All the residents at Candlewick Retirement Community are old. I get that." His eyes narrowed. "But driving a metro bus for twenty-five years, you learn to be observant."

"Really?"

"Think about it. All day long, year in, year out, driving a giant vehicle through narrow lanes of traffic, needing to watch for all the idiots buzzing around with no regard for human safety, trying to pass on the wrong side. All day long, complete strangers stepping into your bus. So, you have to keep your eyes on the road and also on the passengers. You have to see what people are doing before they do it."

"But he died of kidney failure. If they thought it was suspicious at all, I'm sure the sheriff or one of his deputies would have been out here asking questions." She inhaled and let out a big breath. "Did you notice something suspicious? If so, you should report it."

Earl shook his head vigorously. "They don't care. Kent is just one more old man who died in a retirement home."

"But if you saw someone murder that poor man. . ." Jenny stopped. "Say, wait a minute. You and I were sitting together the whole time. When would you have even seen this suspicious behavior? Nobody touched George Kent."

"All kinds of people touched him."

"Well, yeah. . ."

"Shook his hand, patted him on the arm, bumped against him in the crowd."

"Sure. But that's not the same as seeing someone stab him."

"I said nothing of the kind."

"But when did you see somebody murder him? And who would do such a thing in front of a whole room of—"

"In front of a whole room full of witnesses?" Earl sat back in his wheelchair and grunted. "Yeah. That's the question."

"So. . ." Her face changed. Her tone of voice reflected her pity. "Are you feeling okay, Mr. Walker?"

The old man glared at her. "This is not some delusion or illusion or whatever the word is." Earl tilted his head one way, then the other. Then he shrugged resignedly. "Look, I don't know what I saw. There was something just not right."

"I see."

Earl perked up. "There is something. The ring was gone."

Jenny sat up. "What ring?"

"After the so-called party, that ring was missing off the coffee table." Earl looked at Jenny. "You know, the one he showed off to you? Everyone was trying to find it."

Her eyes got big. "Oh!" She narrowed them. "I'm sure there's a logical explanation. Maybe someone just took it for safekeeping."

Earl shook his head. "Nobody there was ready to do Kent any favors."

"That's an awfully cold way to look at it."

"Maybe you should open your eyes sometimes. Everybody is cold."

"I don't believe that."

"The sooner you do, the sooner you can grow out of that religion of yours. The sooner you can join the rest of us out here in the real world."

CHAPTER FOUR

The girl left him soon afterward, quietly. Earl tried his best not to think about how he had hurt her feelings. He was finally, wonderfully alone, and he planned to put the whole unpleasantness out of his mind.

However, there seemed to be a cloud of doubt hovering over him as he wheeled himself to the center of the room. He started to reach for the remote on the coffee table but instead grabbed one of the framed photos of his late wife. He stared at Barbara for a long moment. "I know, baby. But there's no percentage in getting involved."

The picture did not answer.

"College gets on my nerves. You always had more patience than me. I would never admit it to her, but when she forced me to get out of the apartment, I was secretly glad. I've been hibernating in this old rattrap for so long I've forgotten how to get out."

The picture didn't answer that, either.

"Of course, the first place she takes me to. . ." He stopped himself and changed the subject. "And I sort of met somebody when we went to the rec center. I hope that's okay with you. Her name is Gloria Logan."

The photograph of Barbara kept smiling. Her black hair framed her face just so.

Earl set his jaw, thrust out his lower lip. His breathing came heavier. "I don't know what to do, Barbara. I can't get involved." He let out a big sigh. "When a man is an island for so long, he can't remember how to connect with the mainland anymore."

He wiped his nose with his sleeve. "Well, you know what I mean." He smiled weakly at the photo. "You always did." He looked at the eyes he remembered so well in his dreams. "I miss you."

Earl set down the photo and got the television remote. He turned on the TV and flipped through the channels. Courtroom show. Trashy news program. Sitcom. *Click, click, click.* He sat in front of the flickering screen for some block of time, but he wouldn't have been able to recall what he watched.

He was almost grateful when there was a knock at the door. After shutting off the TV, he went to the door to find Mark Conroy standing there. Earl said, "Hello. You throw some kind of party." He didn't invite the man in.

"Yes." Conroy forced a grin then dropped it. "I just wanted to check and make sure that you were okay."

"Why wouldn't I be?"

"Well, a few people from the party have been sick today. I just wanted to make sure you were okay."

"I'm fine. We can't say the same for Kent."

"Oh. You heard." Conroy stood in the doorway a few seconds, uncertainly. "By the way, I'm sorry about how Kent crawled all over you there. I hope he didn't cause any damage?"

Earl tilted his head. "No."

"By the way, he dropped something in my apartment—a ring. Maybe you saw it?"

"He showed it off to me. He seemed to show it off to everybody."

"Yes." Conroy nodded. "Anyway, it seems to have been misplaced. You didn't happen to see what happened to it, did you?"

Earl shook his head. "No."

"Well, if it turns up, here is my number." Conroy handed Earl a scrap of paper with a phone number scribbled on it. "As the host, I feel responsible for making sure it gets into the right hands."

Earl nodded. "Okay."

Conroy lingered a moment. Finally he said, "Well, I guess I'll see you around. Glad to hear you didn't get sick."

After Earl closed the door, he went to the end table by the couch and stuck the scrap of paper in the drawer. He considered going back to the TV but changed his mind and made dinner. He was boiling some noodles when there was a knock at the front door. Wondering how in the world he suddenly got so popular, he pulled the pot off the burner and went to see who it was.

Sally Brouwer was at the door. "Um, hi."

Earl nodded. "Hello."

"I didn't know if you heard, but some people got sick at the party yesterday."

"I also heard that a man died."

"Oh—yes. That was a shame. Speaking of Kent, did you happen to see what happened to that ring of his?"

Earl forced himself to keep a blank expression on his face. He shook his head thoughtfully. "No, I don't think I did."

"Because he collapsed over around where you—"

"Yeah, I remember. But I don't know what happened to the ring. I guess it must be valuable?"

Sally nodded. "I want to make sure his family gets it."

"That's very kind of you."

"Well, it's already such a tragedy and all. And since Kent wasn't wearing it when he got sick like that, I would hate for it to get lost in the shuffle."

"That is very considerate of you."

"If you happen to remember anything, here is my number." She handed him a neatly folded piece of paper.

Earl nodded and smiled. "Thank you."

After she left, he deposited the number in the end table drawer and finished boiling his noodles. The results were rubbery, which he blamed on the interruption. Although, to be honest, he didn't really know if it was that or his poor cooking.

After dinner he tried to find something to read. Perusing all the materials within arm's reach, he went through his options: the Candlewick newsletter, the newspaper, a biography of Winston Churchill, a book on World War II, a self-help book, and an encyclopedia of celebrity pets. Earl could not for the life of him remember how he had ended up with that last one.

He settled on the biography of Churchill. However, the words just seemed to float around him. That weird feeling continued to gnaw at Earl's concentration. Something at that party had not been right. There was no evidence of any crime—by all accounts, George Kent was just an old man who should have watched his diet more carefully and died for his carelessness. But something about the whole scene just did not sit right with Earl.

He tried his best to concentrate on the book in his hands. Finally, after reading the same paragraph multiple times, he gave up.

Maybe it was time to get ready for bed. Because—and he could not be any clearer about this to himself—he was not going to get involved. No matter how much the matter of Kent's death weighed on his mind. He wheeled himself to the bathroom sink, reaching for the railing on the wall and pulling himself to a standing position, careful to avoid eye contact with the man facing him in the mirror.

What are you so nervous about? You're not going to get involved. There's no reason for you to be nervous.

In the dark, the faded light from the next room illuminated his face in the mirror. The man looking back at him was so old. For some reason it surprised him.

He leaned on his palms against the sink. "I just need some sleep. That's all." Yeah, that was it. Everything would be different in the morning.

Getting himself back into his wheelchair, he wheeled to the dresser and got out some fresh pajamas. His hands trembled. He didn't talk to himself all through the process of changing for bed.

By the time he finally made it to bed, he thought the matter was resolved. His plan was to close his eyes and fall into blissful unconsciousness. All would be well in the morning.

Earl did not count on not being able to sleep. Staring at the ceiling, he talked to the darkness. "Look, there is no reason to talk to the cops." The darkness didn't answer. "After all, why would they believe me? Even College decided I was crazy."

Earl's mind wandered. He kept replaying the afternoon of the party in his head. The girl's visit. How he badgered her into dusting. How she badgered him into getting out of the apartment.

His memories flickered to the bowling game. How the entire room stopped when George Kent walked through. Everyone who knew George Kent lived in fear of him.

He thought of the party afterward. Everyone had played nice.

But everyone hated Kent. But someone liked him enough to give him a box of cigars. (Where did he get those again?) Someone thought enough of him to bring him grape juice. (Who was that again?) Someone liked him enough to bring him chili. (Where had that come from again?) And someone had apparently taken his ring.

Earl twitched. "I'm in no position to judge," he told the darkness. He hoped it passed no judgment.

But he couldn't stop thinking. About the cigars. The grape juice. The chili. The ring.

It was obvious he was not going to get any sleep this way. Earl clapped his hands and the lamp came on. He checked the clock. It was after eleven. He sat up, wondering how to occupy himself. He hadn't been up this late in years.

First he boiled some water. Not for tea. Not for coffee. Just for the hot water. The whole process took maybe twenty minutes. He tried to focus on the water as it started to bubble, then boil furiously. He poured it into a cup and drank it as fast as his throat would allow. The cup of hot, clear liquid soothed his stomach somewhat.

But it failed to do anything about the images eating at the back of his mind.

"I just need some air," he told himself. He toyed with just going out in his pajamas and maybe his robe but quickly dismissed the idea. So he went to the trouble of changing into his shirt and pants. He pulled on his slippers and wheeled to the door.

Outside in the common garden, Earl stopped and sniffed the honeysuckle. He thought about how much Barbara had loved the stuff. He wondered whether Gloria liked it.

Earl decided he needed to wander. Most folks would call it "taking a walk" or "taking a stroll." Even after all these years in a wheelchair, he still wasn't sure what he should call it. Maybe "taking a spin."

Whatever it was, Earl let his mind go blank as he simply let his hands and wheels take him wherever. The trick was to not think. Not to let any of the recent unpleasantness get to him. The way that man bullied his way into the bowling tournament. The chili party. The way all those old fools lapped up the food.

The cigars.

The grape juice.

The chili.

The ring.

"Stop that," Earl grumbled to himself. "You've got to just stop thinking about it."

Stop thinking about the man on the floor, his life probably leaking out of his body even as they all watched.

With a jolt, Earl suddenly noticed where he was. His eyes adjusting to the nighttime lighting, he recognized the hall where the caravan had gone to Mark Conroy's chili party. And that door there—right there—was where Kent had talked with Nelson. Where Nelson had handed Kent the box of cigars. Kent had gone inside.

Earl sat. Earl pondered. Earl heard a crash.

His inclination was to simply turn and wheel away. It was none of his business.

But he couldn't. He looked both ways down the empty hallway. He looked again at Kent's apartment door. Maybe he just imagined the noise.

Crash. There was definitely someone inside, breaking things.

Scratching the side of his nose, Earl wondered what to do.

Clang. Earl wheeled right up to the door and started to reach for the knob. He stopped himself, literally grabbed one hand with the other. What did he think he was doing?

There was no telling who was behind that door. What if he was up to no good? He was probably carrying a crowbar. Or a baseball bat. Maybe a gun or a machete.

And here Earl was just a crippled old man in a wheelchair. It wouldn't take much to knock him senseless or simply tip his chair over, step over him, and run away.

Earl was humiliated to be faced with his own helplessness.

Smash. He considered knocking on the nearby doors, but he had no idea who lived along this row of apartments. Banging on random doors could be just a waste of time, and he was in a hurry. Making up his mind, Earl gripped the wheels of his chair and turned in the direction of Candlewick's front desk—maybe someone was on duty.

On the way to the front desk, Earl got turned around a few times. The second time he passed the chapel, he got reoriented. When he made it to his destination, the entrance to the lobby was dark. Just the running lights were on.

The desk was unmanned. Earl licked his lips, tried to control his breathing. "Hello?" His voice came out a hoarse whisper. He cleared his throat and tried again. "Is anyone here?"

A voice singsonged from behind a closed door. "Just a second." After a moment the door opened. It was the young man from before—what was his name? Oh yeah, Grant Caine. The kid broke into a grin when he saw Earl. "Hello, sir! Lost your way again?"

"I came to report a burglary."

Concern shadowed Caine's face. "A what?"

Earl pointed back down the hall from which he had come. "There is somebody in Kent's apartment right now."

Now the kid was puzzled. "Kent who?"

"George Kent, the guy who keeled over yesterday. Somebody is tearing up his apartment right now."

The kid was slow. "There is somebody in George—"

"Shouldn't you be snapping to action right now? Paging the security guard or something?"

"Right. Right." Caine ran his fingers through his brown hair. He looked right at Earl. "We've got to do something."

"That's what I've been saying!"

"So, you were in Mr. Kent's apartment, and you think you saw—"

"I was out in the hall. I heard some intruder in the apartment."

Caine looked at Earl doubtfully. "Maybe you just imagined it."

Earl gritted his teeth. "I did not imagine it." Hands on his wheels he turned toward the desk. There had to be a telephone.

Ah. There.

He jumped at the receiver and held it out to Caine, stretching the cord to its limit. "Call someone. Security. The president. Dick Tracy. I don't care who."

"Right." Caine was nodding now. Earl didn't know what College saw in him. The kid took the phone. "Right." He hesitated then started searching an address book on the desk. "I'll have to see what Mr. Nelson says. He's the director."

"Now we're talking."

Caine jabbed his finger at an item in the book then punched the numbers into the phone. He waited for it to ring through. There was another voice on the line. Earl couldn't hear it distinctly, but he assumed it was Ed Nelson. Probably interrupted at home, unhappy to be disturbed. Caine responded. "Hello, sir? Sorry to call you this time of night, but there has been an alleged, um, noise. One of the residents may have heard something in one of the residential units."

"I know what I heard," Earl snapped. He could hear the man on the other end of the line bark some orders. From the wince on the boy's face, Caine was being chewed out for interrupting the man's sleep or his television show or something. Caine nodded at whatever the man was saying. "Yes, sir. Of course, sir. I'll get right on it."

He hung up the phone and looked at Earl started to say something, but no words came out. Then he turned and ran.

CHAPTER ⛩ FIVE

The kid was almost out of sight before it registered with Earl that he had been left behind. Hands on his wheels, he decided to follow. He had the disadvantages of (1) being tired from all the earlier excitement; (2) not being as fast as the young man; and (3) not being able to quite remember his way back.

Making a vow to soon sit down with some sort of map of Candlewick Retirement Community, he made a mental note to become fully acquainted with the exact layout of the place—if only for the few days left before the place was shut down forever.

The second time Earl passed the chapel, he reoriented himself and was on his way. Probably. About two-thirds of the way there, he had to stop. His hands were starting to cramp. This was more activity than he'd had in, well, years.

He could imagine the scene of the crime. There would be a scuffle. Maybe a full-blown fight. Did the boy have the stuff to defend himself?

Waiting to catch his breath, resting his hands, Earl wondered what in the world he thought he was doing. What if he got to the scene there and the kid was involved in some sort of karate fight? What good could an old man in a wheelchair do? He was in no condition to back the boy up.

In the old days he could have helped big time. Back when he was a metro bus driver, Earl had the stuff to take care of troublemakers. That is, until. . .

But look at him now. Broken-down. Defeated. Just a grumpy, withered, lonely old man in a wheelchair. What did he have to offer anyone? Really?

By the time Earl found his way back to Kent's apartment, the door was open. Light streamed into the dark hallway. Earl stopped his chair short of the door. He looked this way and that, making sure the coast was clear. That young man, Caine, was nowhere to be seen.

Earl heard a gruff voice cut into the darkness. "What's goings on out here?" One of the doors had opened after all, an old man standing there. Earl did not recognize him. The man demanded, "Do I gotta calls the cops?"

"Mind your own business," Earl grumbled.

The man, halfway out his apartment door, stood in his robe and fluffy slippers. Earl didn't want to think what might (or might not) be under that ragged terrycloth robe. The man pointed at Earl. "What's all the noises out here?"

Earl raised his eyebrows. "You heard something? Did you see who it was? Perhaps somebody dressed in black?" He squinted. "Maybe a foreigner?"

The apartment door across the way opened. A woman's voice cracked, "What's all the fuss?"

The man pointed at Earl. "This fella's makings all kindsa racket."

"I am not!" Controlling his tone of voice, Earl tried again. "Ma'am, I was just passing by. Now, maybe if this gentleman could—"

"Like fun," the man said. "I hears the noise, I wents and gots my glasses, and then I looks out the window and sees you right here." The man shook his fist at Earl. "Now, knocks off the noise so some people can gets some sleep!"

Earl turned his attention to the woman, her gray hair exploding in frizz. "I am just an innocent bystander." Seeing her notice the wheelchair, Earl added with a forced chuckle, "So to speak." He pointed at the other man. "This gentleman here seems to have heard some sort of disturbance and, instead of getting his facts straight, thought it would be easier to accuse—"

The man in the doorway cursed. "Fine. Fine." He nodded, shifting his weight from one foot to the other, like winding himself up to start moving again. "I'm gonna calls the police force." He shut the door.

The lady let out an exasperated sigh. "He will, you know. You had best be gone before he comes back out to ask you for your description."

Earl looked at the man's closed door, then he turned his attention back to the woman. "What do you mean by that?"

"He can't see so well."

Earl frowned. "Thanks." So much for hoping for a witness. He gripped the wheels of his chair. His fingers still ached, but he needed to get out of the hall before they woke the whole complex up.

Inching carefully toward the open door of Kent's apartment, Earl peeked inside. The place was a mess. Furniture turned at strange angles, cushions and knickknacks scattered on the carpet. When he saw the youngster, Earl allowed a sigh of relief to escape. "Whew. He didn't knock you out."

The kid was poking around. "Who didn't?"

"The burglar."

The kid shook his head. "The place is empty. Nobody was here."

Earl's heart fell. "But I heard them."

Caine looked at Earl and pursed his lips. "When I got here, the door was wide open. And look at this mess. Unless. . ." He looked at Earl. "This isn't how he kept the place, is it?"

"How should I know?"

"Well, you knew this gentleman, didn't you? I mean, you all lived here at Candlewick."

"No." Earl gritted his teeth. "I did not know him. But I was at the gathering where he, um, expired."

The boy frowned back. "And you came into his apartment for some sense of closure?"

"I was not in here."

"But the door was wide open."

Earl fidgeted in his chair. Was it just him? "Okay, let's go back to the beginning. The door here was closed. I was in the hall out there. I heard the noise. I came to see you. Here you are."

Caine stared back at Earl, slack jawed. As the silence grew, Earl coughed. "End of story." The boy continued to stare. Earl added, "Because, you know. Here you are. And so am I."

"Uh-huh."

Earl squinted. "So you didn't see anybody when you got here?"

"Nope. The door was wide open. Wide open. Nobody here." The kid's pocket started to play music. He pulled out his cell phone and checked the caller ID. "It's Mr. Nelson." He opened the phone. "Hello?"

The kid listened to his cell phone intently, nodding to whatever was being said on the other end. He put his hand over his other ear then stepped out of the apartment altogether.

Alone, Earl looked at the mess around him. What in the world could the intruder have been looking for? The couch was pulled out from the wall. The cushions were thrown aside. All the furniture had been shoved into the middle of the living room. Framed items had been yanked off their wall hooks and dropped onto the carpet. Drawers were pulled out, cabinet doors opened. The shelves were cleared, everything shoved to the floor.

This was not a robbery.

He turned his chair and wheeled for the door, maneuvering around the scatter. He was working his way around a misplaced end table when his right wheel caught on something. An object. On the floor.

Earl looked down to navigate around it and saw it was a metal box. Some sort of strongbox, by the look of it. He stretched for it, but reaching the floor from here was tough. He leaned hard and got his fingertips on it but just could not grasp it.

You're working awfully hard for a man who doesn't want to get involved. Earl sat back up. He glanced at the door and saw the coast was still clear. So he looked around for something to use—a broom, a golf club, anything long would do. For lack of any better available tools, Earl wheeled over to a nearby potted plant and dragged it back across the room. It took him a few jerks to coordinate the whole process with his chair.

Gripping the plant as low as he could, Earl swung it so that the pot clunked the metal box toward him. The metal box now on its side, Earl reached again. The plant came out of the pot, roots and all, loose dirt dumping out on the carpet. Earl was unhappy to add to the mess, but Kent was not likely to complain now.

Earl dropped the plant. Pulling the box onto his lap, he brushed off the dirt. But he did not have to wonder about the contents of the box—because it was already pried open.

It was full of money. Cash. Long green.

Confused, Earl looked around the room again. Whoever had broken into the apartment had found this box, pried it open— and left all this money behind.

Was the intruder scared off? Or was he looking for something else?

Earl hesitated again, trying to think what he should do with all this money. He could trust it to the kid. No—who knew where he might lose it? Give it to someone in the Candlewick office. Who knew whether those people were trustworthy?

No. Earl needed to think on this one. He needed to take the box home for safekeeping, where he could give the matter some serious, careful thought.

Glancing again at the front door, he pulled up his afghan and stashed the box on his lap. He lowered the afghan.

His curiosity now full bore, Earl looked around the living room with new eyes. If the burglar did not want the metal box, then what was he really looking for? What in this place would be more valuable—or more important—than a box full of money?

He glanced from wall to wall. There would be no wall safes— the walls at Candlewick were too thin for anything like that.

Earl looked at the carpet, now covered with piles of loose dirt. Maybe something hidden under the carpet? Not so far as Earl could see.

Giving up on finding anything else of use in the living room, Earl wheeled to the kitchenette. All manner of plastic containers had been pulled out of the fridge and set on the counter, on the stove, on every flat surface. Someone had opened everything, the flour, the ice cream, the peanut butter—everything.

Wheeling his way into the man's bedroom, Earl gasped anew. The bed was overturned, the mattress flipped this way, the box springs that. All the dresser drawers had been yanked out and dumped on the floor. The dresser was pulled out from the wall, the mirror flipped over.

Earl saw a row of open-top boxes placed along the floor against the wall, chock-full of classic long-playing records. Apparently the intruder had been scared off before he or she had gotten to these. Earl looked at the spines and saw an assortment of Frank Sinatra, Louis Prima, and Mel Torme. Something about the collection connected with Earl in a way he would not have expected. Maybe he and Kent had some common ground after all. If things had been different. . .

Earl grimaced. Things were not different. Things were exactly how they were.

He was turning to go when he noticed something. Earl looked at the record collection again. Looked around the bedroom. Whirled the chair around once, twice. He looked at the LPs again. Wheeled into the other room, got to the living room. Looked around him, at the various types of furniture and appliances.

"Oh man, what happened over here?" It was the kid, back in the apartment, looking at the dirt all over the front carpet. "I can't believe they did this."

Earl grunted but didn't confess anything.

The kid looked up. "That was the managing director. We need to leave here now."

"Why?"

"He doesn't want us to touch anything until he can get here."

CHAPTER SIX

When he awoke the next day, Earl spent all morning ignoring the metal box. He was determined to put the entire business out of his mind, and so spent all morning thinking about how he was not going to think about it.

His hands and arms were stiff from the exertion of the night before. How could he have gotten involved like that? The question triggered memories of that fateful day on the bus. He shivered and tried to think of something else.

No interesting topics came to mind. At least none that did not lead around back to that metal box. So Earl threw back the covers and got up for the day. Went through his whole morning routine, all the while patting himself on the back for not thinking about the box.

He got to his breakfast—a bowl of cereal, six lemon-flavored prunes, and a glass of orange juice. He preferred grapefruit juice, but it interfered with his meds. Earl checked his pill schedule, took the appropriate pills, and finished his cereal dry.

During the whole process, his hands and arms ached. He wondered whether he might have pulled something in his shoulder.

He flipped on the TV and tried to watch the morning news, but he couldn't focus. He flipped around the channels for a bit, trying to find something, anything, to occupy him. It didn't work.

He finally broke down and admitted to himself that if he didn't want to think about the metal box, he should not have sneaked it home. As the morning sun peeked through the crack in the curtain, Earl tried to remember his state of mind the night before.

Who was that old man in the wheelchair who got involved? "Oh, that's right," he grumbled to himself. "That was you." It wasn't the Earl Walker he knew. Not the Earl Walker he knew at all.

Clutching the round dining table, he pushed himself up and followed the railing around to the refrigerator. He pushed aside the ketchup, the pitcher of water, the half-empty jar of bread and butter pickles, and reached for the gray metal box stuck in the back. It was cold. The fridge might not have been the perfect hiding place, but it was all he could think of at the time. It worked, didn't it? Nobody broke in and found it there.

Wheeling himself into the living room by the lamp, he set the cold box on the coffee table then sat back and looked at it. The only scratches were around the lock. Had the intruder broken it open, or had Kent done that himself?

Reaching for the box, Earl flipped it open. A thought shot through him, and he looked at his fingers, then wheeled to the kitchenette for a towel and some cleanser. He was about to spray down the box when he stopped himself. Was it better to have his fingerprints on this box or not? After all, he had nothing to hide. Would wiping down the box make it look like he did?

"Let's think this through," Earl said aloud. "If a burglar had left fingerprints on this box, that could be important evidence." He rubbed his chin. "Then again, if said criminal person was thoughtless enough to leave prints on this box, he would have also left his prints all over that apartment."

Not to mention, by now Earl had probably already obliterated any useful prints. He looked at the box now, the lid open, the stack of money right there. If the sheriff showed up right now, at this moment, how would he explain that?

"I'll just explain it calmly," Earl said out loud. "It belongs to George Kent's family. With all manner of intruders coming and going at will, it made no sense to leave such valuable property out in the open. Right?"

It sounded good, so he went along and agreed with himself.

And as he was making an inventory for the sake of Kent's family, it stood to reason that he would have to make an assessment of its contents. And if in the process a few of his own questions might be answered, so much the better.

Besides, what if the money got tied up somewhere as "evidence"? Tagged and boxed and stuck in storage somewhere, until the sheriff tracked down the intruder or burglar and brought him to trial? Or worse, what if the box of money somehow fell through the cracks and got lost in the system? That hardly seemed fair to the family.

So, it was settled: For the time being, Earl would not volunteer the existence of the box to anybody. He would not lie if directly asked, but there was no point in bringing it up unnecessarily.

He wondered what Barbara would have said to that. He put it out of his mind.

Turning his attention to the actual contents inside the box, it certainly did seem like a lot of money. Earl pulled out the stacks of bills. What was this, hundreds of dollars? Thousands? Flipping through them, he saw groupings of fives, tens, twenties, and hundreds. After he added it up, he whistled aloud. Why in the world would the man keep so much money on hand?

But Earl's mind kept circling back around to an even more nagging question: Why would a burglar have left so much money behind?

There was a knock at the door. Earl's first instinct was to hide the box. It could be the authorities at the door, finally coming to get his statement. "Be right there!"

He flipped the lid closed and slid the box off the table into his lap. He considered taking it all the way back to the fridge, but that would take him too long. And he didn't want it to seem like he was hiding something. Especially since he was, in fact, hiding something.

He dropped the box on the floor and pushed it under the couch and wheeled himself to the door. He took a second to catch his breath, compose himself, and slap a more casual expression on his face. Then he fumbled with the knob and opened the door.

Gloria Logan stood there. "Hello, Blue Eyes."

"Oh. Hi." His heart beat faster. It annoyed him.

She stood in the doorway awkwardly. "I didn't hear from you. I was worried."

"You didn't hear from me? When did you ever hear from me?" It was actually gruffer than Earl intended, but he was anxious to get back to the mysterious box under the couch.

Gloria rubbed her fingers nervously. "Well, I mean, nobody has seen you around. So I wanted to make sure you were doing okay. After everything that happened."

"After. . . ?" Had news of the burglary gotten around?

"Well, you know, at the party. George Kent dropping dead and all."

"Oh. Of course." Earl remembered his manners. "Would you like to come in? Can I get you something? Coffee? Juice?"

"I guess I could spare a few minutes for a cup of coffee."

"Oh. Um, I haven't actually made any." Earl felt his face grow warm. "Sorry, I just asked out of habit. I used to make coffee for Barbara, my late wife." He glanced toward the couch, then back. "I'm sorry. I wasn't prepared for visitors."

She offered a wobbly smile. "I need to get going anyway. I was just passing by." Gloria stood another second, lingering.

He sat awkwardly, unable to think of anything to say. He stopped himself from looking back at the couch again.

Finally Gloria said, "Maybe we can talk later?"

"Sure."

"Here is my number if you need to reach me for anything." She handed him a slip of paper.

After she was gone, Earl closed the door and pulled the chain. It took him some doing to retrieve the gray metal box from under the couch.

Setting it back on the coffee table, he flipped open the lid and marveled again at the contents inside. "Why would George Kent have this much cash on hand?" Earl did not wait for the empty apartment to answer. He reached for the rubber banded stacks and pulled them out one at a time. They made quite a pile on the table.

Where had the money come from? And why hadn't the man stored it in some safe place? It was all so strange.

Of course, the real question was whether this was connected

with Kent's death. And what about Kent's precious ring? Had whoever stolen the ring needed something from Kent's apartment? Was there some secret engraved inside the metal band—maybe the combination to a safe or a riddle that led to a treasure?

"You are losing it, Earl," he told himself. And frankly, he was inclined to agree with himself. Seriously, a treasure?

At the bottom of the box, Earl found a little black book. At first he was hesitant to open it. If this was a collection of women's phone numbers, then it was none of his business.

Then Earl remembered how Kent had talked to Gloria. If that was how he behaved when the two of them were in public. . . He immediately flipped the book open and began to search it, telling himself that he was merely looking for clues. There were lots of names, but the numerical figures ascribed to each one did not look like telephone numbers.

Some names seemed familiar, but no "Kent" was listed. It would have been nice if the book had listed some family members, maybe Kent's children or grandchildren—or even a lawyer who might be handling Kent's estate—but nothing in the entries indicated what relationship Kent had with each person.

Of course, the authorities no doubt had resources to track such people down. And speaking of authorities, why had no one shown up yet?

He should have never gotten involved. It was easier to simply shrink more into his shell and hope the situation would pass. He had learned his lesson about getting involved years ago, on his last day as a bus driver. It was a lesson he had held tightly to in the years since, even as he drifted further away from contact with the outside world.

You say the state of Kentucky is forcing all the residents of

Candlewick Retirement Community to find new places to live? Shrink more into the shell and hope the problem goes away.

You say George Kent died in front of a room full of witnesses under mysterious circumstances? Further into the shell.

But all these mental gymnastics were a lot of fancy dancing around the central question: How did Kent get all this money? There was something about the way the money was arranged, something about the names and numbers in the book, combined with Earl's general impression of the man when he was still alive. It was hard not to assume it all pointed to something bad.

A furious pounding on his door interrupted his thoughts. Earl gripped his wheels, rocking his chair forward and back a couple times. He turned and yelled at the door in a cracked voice, "J–just a minute!"

It had to be the sheriff. He looked at the table. Scrambling, he threw the money into the metal box. He tried to close the lid, but the money had not been stacked neatly enough. Of course, the lock was broken anyway. He shoved it back under the couch.

Getting to the door, he stopped his chair. Put his hand to his chest, forced himself to breathe normally. He closed his eyes, waited a moment for the spots to clear.

Okay.

Okay.

Wait—wait.

Okay.

He reached for the knob, opened the door.

College was standing there, distraught, on edge. "Where have you been?"

"Oh. Um, I was just—"

"Grant was fired! And it's all your fault!"

CHAPTER SEVEN

E arl frowned. "What are you talking about?"

Jenny pressed through the doorway, made her way to the couch, and sat down. "They said he was helping you with something last night, and then this morning they fired him!"

"Maybe you misunderstood." He nervously glanced toward the box's hiding place. It was sitting right behind the girl's shoes. "I'm sure he was laid off because Candlewick is closing down. You know, we residents aren't the only ones being put out on the street. When this place shuts down, all the employees are gone, too."

"No—I was at the front desk, and I happened to ask about Grant. And the man working up there said he was fired because some old man in a wheelchair called the county sheriff on him!"

"I was not the one who called the sheriff!" Earl averted his eyes. "I told your friend to."

Her eyes grew wide, and she pointed. "They *were* talking about you!" She set her jaw. "What did you do?"

Earl looked at her. "Well, the sheriff will surely be here any minute to ask about it. I guess there's no harm in telling you, too." He outlined most of the events of the previous evening, careful to leave out any mention of the box of money. "I wonder what's keeping the sheriff anyway. I may be an old man, but I'm still a witness."

"Maybe you could go to the office and say something," the girl said. "Demand they give Grant his job back."

Earl rubbed his chin. Who did the kid call? That's right, Candlewick's managing director, Ed Nelson. The same man Earl saw talking with George Kent just hours before the man died. Earl locked his fingers together and looked at Jenny. Pretended to smile. "Fine. If it will make you happy, I'll go talk to the managing director himself."

"Thank you."

"Say, maybe you can help me with a problem."

Jenny tilted her head uncertainly. "What?"

"Say a man has collected a lot of money—maybe his life savings—but he doesn't trust banks. He wants to keep the money close by for some reason. Where would he keep it?"

"Mr. Walker, if you want to change to another bank, I can help you with—"

"No," Earl snapped, annoyed. "It is not me."

"So, this really is a 'friend' you're talking about?"

"It's not me."

"Of course."

"I'm not talking hypothetically. This is an actual person."

"Fine."

"Are you going to help me or not?"

Jenny chuckled. "Lessee. . .and this certain man doesn't want to put his money in a regular bank?"

"Maybe he had some bad experience with the bank. Or maybe he has some other reason not to keep it there."

"You know, banks today are insured."

"I know, I know, I'm just saying what-if."

She sat back, thinking. "Hmm. I guess I've heard of folks who have pasted it on the walls and then covered it up with wallpaper."

"Yikes! That's crazy!"

"I didn't say it was a smart thing to do. I just said I heard about it."

"Fine." Earl rubbed his hands together. "Okay, that's one."

She frowned. "You don't want to do that."

"It's not me."

"Right. I forgot." She thought for another second. "And you can stuff it inside the mattress."

"Of course. The mattress. Okay, that's two."

She sat forward, getting into it. "Or maybe inside the wall, and you plaster over it. Or bury it in the backyard."

Earl shook his head. "If you're living in an apartment, you really can't put it inside the wall."

"Yeah, I guess management would complain about it."

"Actually, it's more like, if you push something into the wall, you're really shoving it into the next apartment."

"Oh. I see what you mean. And you don't want to bury it out in the yard, because anyone could find it out there. A dog might dig it up, or the groundskeeper would certainly run into it, sooner or later."

"Exactly." Earl nodded. He squinted, his eyes staring nowhere in particular. He mumbled, "So why not a box?"

"I'm sorry, what box?"

"I just find it interesting that you didn't say, 'Put the money in a box.'"

"Well, I suppose you could get, like, a safe deposit box or

something." Jenny looked at him squarely. "What is all this about?"

Earl shook his head. "No, not a safe deposit box. This man doesn't want to put it in a bank, remember?"

"He could always change his mind. People can do that."

A little late for this guy, Earl thought.

Jenny changed the subject. "So, when are you going to the office to straighten everything out for Grant?"

He sighed. "The boy needed to find a new job anyway."

"But this will look bad on his resume."

The two got turned around in the hall. By the second time they passed the general store, they had it figured out. They passed the scene of the crime—the second crime, that is, if in fact it were ever proven there had been a first crime—but there was no sign that there had been any sort of untoward activity the night before. No forensic professionals dusting for prints. No guard dogs. No yellow tape.

Earl looked up at College, who was intently pushing his chair. Apparently she had no idea they were even passing the apartment in question, and he wasn't going to bring it up.

When they finally reached the office for Candlewick Retirement Community, Gloria Logan was behind the desk. "Well, hello there, Blue Eyes! Long time no see!"

Earl shrank back in his chair. "Um. Hi."

Jenny gave a little wave. "Hello, ma'am. What a nice surprise, finding you here!"

Gloria patted her hair. "I work here in the office part-time, you know, to help out. How are you doing, darlin'?"

"I'm well, thanks." Jenny dismissed the topic with a wave. "I guess there was some big excitement this morning, huh?"

The older woman batted her big eyelashes. "Whatever could you mean?"

"You know, with the sheriff and all."

"What? The sheriff is coming here?" Gloria started to rise up from her chair.

Earl grunted. "Actually, we thought he would have been here already."

"Are you all right?" Gloria's eyes were wide. Earl noticed they were almost the same shade of brown as Barbara's had been. She asked Earl, "Why didn't you say something this morning?"

Jenny jumped in. "Mr. Walker witnessed a robber or something—" She stopped. "Wait—this morning?"

"Burglar," Earl said. "If the victim is right there, the bad guy is called a 'robber'; if the victim is not there, you call him a 'burglar.' "

Jenny took in a breath and started over. "Last night Mr. Walker heard a—criminal—and reported it to Grant Caine." Jenny blushed. "You know, that young man who. . ."

Gloria smiled at Jenny. "I know who you mean, dear."

"And then Grant and Mr. Walker both went back to the scene of the robbery—"

"Burglary."

"—burglary, and the, er, assailant was gone."

"Ooh, *assailant*," Earl said. "But I don't think they actually assaulted anyone."

Ignoring him, Jenny pressed on. "And now this morning I was coming to visit Mr. Walker, and I thought I would swing by first and say hello to, um—" She blushed again.

Gloria smiled at her again. "I know what you mean."

Jenny's face went hard. "And then I find out he was fired!"

The other woman's eyes went wide again. Yes, Earl thought, the exact shade of brown. She asked, "He was?"

"Yes," Jenny said, obviously unaffected by the woman's brown eyes.

Earl held up his hands. "Which I had nothing to do with." He heard College sputter, but he cut her off. "Just the same, it might be a good idea to talk to the manager."

"Mr. Nelson?" Gloria seemed worried. "Are you sure? I mean, about there being an intruder? And this young man was somehow involved? He always seemed so nice."

Jenny cut in. "We're here to get him his job back!"

"I see." Gloria tilted her head and frowned. Clearly she did not see at all. Not that Earl could blame her—this story was clearly jumping around too much for the casual observer to be able to follow. She just said, "Okay, I'll check with Mr. Nelson." She looked in the appointment book on her desk then got up and went into another room.

Jenny and Earl waited.

When Gloria returned, she gave them an apologetic shrug. "Mr. Nelson will see you in a few minutes. Can I get you some coffee? And I actually have some here." She winked at Earl.

He resisted the urge to squirm. "Sure."

She looked at Jenny, who nodded. "Some coffee would be great, thanks."

"Cream, sugar?" Both nodded.

As Gloria left for the back, Jenny whispered, "See, I told you she likes you. She called you 'Sugar.'"

"No, she asked if we wanted sugar in our coffee."

"That's not what it sounded like to me. She said, 'Cream, sugar?'"

"No, she said, 'Cream? Sugar?' Two nouns, separated by a question mark." Earl tried his best to sound convinced, but he did feel some sort of flutter in his chest.

Gloria returned and gave each a Styrofoam cup of brown liquid, flecks of white stuff floating on top. Jenny asked, "So you live at Candlewick, but you also work at Candlewick?"

"Two days a week. I guess I could give you the nickel tour."

Earl, sipping his coffee, resisted the urge to wipe his mouth with his sleeve. "Sure."

Gloria gestured to take in the items on top of her desk. "This is, of course, my desk area. Here's my blotter—although I guess nobody really blots anything anymore, unless you count the coffee I've spilled on it." She chuckled.

Earl just stared. "Uh-huh."

She went on. "And here is the phone. It has multiple lines."

"Uh-huh."

Gloria gestured toward a filing cabinet. "And those are the files for all the residents here."

Earl pointed. "So, can just anyone come in and get at those?"

"Of course not!" Gloria seemed to have trouble accepting the concept. But she warmed a bit and added, "That is, all of your information is safely locked up."

"The drawers are always locked?"

"Well," she said tentatively, "they are always either attended or locked." She waved her hand. "I mean, there's never a time when an outsider can just come in and look at your files. So you do not have to worry about that."

"Okay then."

Jenny asked, "So what all do you do here?"

"Oh, the usual. Answer the phone, take messages, make copies, keep track of paperwork. . . ." She nodded. "Office things." She went to a tall metal cabinet and tried to open the doors. Then she snapped her fingers, went to her purse, got out some keys, and unlocked the cabinet.

"And here, of course," she continued, waving her hands like a model on *The Price Is Right*, "are all the office supplies you could ever need." She pointed out the various things as she began itemizing them out loud. "Paper clips. Pens. Pencils. Mailing labels. Copy machine toner. Fluid. Markers. Paper. Folders. Envelopes."

Gloria locked the cabinet back up, returned to her desk, and looked at Earl and Jenny. "So, there was some excitement last night, huh? You weren't hurt, were you?"

Earl hesitated then shook his head. "No."

"But he broke into your home?"

Jenny jumped in. "He was at George Kent's apartment."

Earl shot the college girl an angry look.

Gloria's face went white. "At George's. . ." She looked down at her desk, watching her fingers lock and unlock in different combinations. "That was such a shame Saturday." Her fingers stopped fiddling, and she looked back at Earl. "And you were in his apartment last night?"

"Actually, I was out in the hall." He felt the need to elaborate, so he added, "I was restless and just needed to go out for some air."

Gloria nodded. "Uh-huh." There was an unspoken question in her voice.

Earl continued. "I heard something, and then ran—well, *wheeled*—for the front desk and reported it. I'm surprised the county sheriff hasn't asked me about it by now."

Jenny said, "Maybe he didn't want to bother you. He thought it was better to just let you rest." She looked at Gloria for confirmation.

"Right? The sheriff didn't actually need to talk to him?"

The other woman looked confused. "I told you, I didn't hear anything about it. I haven't seen any kind of police here this morning." She looked at her hands, the fingers twiddling again. "This has all been so. . ." She stopped. "Candlewick has always been so peaceful. Then there was that awful incident at the party, and then George died. And now to hear that somebody may have broken into his apartment. It's hard to feel safe anymore."

"Now, there's no reason to worry," Earl said. "There's probably an explanation." Jenny and Gloria both looked at him, and he realized they expected him to continue. "Oh. Well, for instance, Kent collapsed at the party. It was only natural for his loved ones to be concerned—maybe someone from his family was just looking for some of his things. Some important family documents." Saying it out loud, Earl realized this probably was the explanation—a member of Kent's family. No reason to be alarmed.

Jenny looked at him. "You think so?"

"Sure, that's it." For a second, he almost believed it. But wait—why would a member of his family throw all the furniture around? Or finding a box of money, leave it behind? He looked at Gloria. "Do you know any of Kent's family? Maybe the executor of his estate? I was thinking of sending a card."

Gloria shook her head. "I don't know." She got up and went to the file cabinets along the wall. Reached for the drawer, stopped, and went back to her purse and pulled out her key. She held it up for Earl and laughed. "See?" She went back to the file cabinet, unlocked it, and pulled open the second drawer. She flipped through its contents until she found the folder she wanted and pulled it out. Putting on some reading glasses, she ran a finger along the top sheet of paper. "Um, let's see. . . ." She bit her lip as she read from it.

Watching Gloria, Earl felt something again in his chest. He tried to ignore it.

"Yes," Gloria said, looking up. "I mean, no, he has no family that we know of."

Jenny let out a sympathetic squeal. "He doesn't have any family at all?"

Gloria looked at the file again, adjusting her glasses. "None listed. No next of kin. Even the emergency contact is here at Candlewick."

Earl perked up. "Who?"

"That's funny," Gloria said, reading it. "It says that it's Dandy Anderson."

"Who?"

"You met him at the bowling tournament." Gloria leaned in and whispered loudly. "He was the one who lost that bet."

"Really?"

"I wonder why he didn't list Mark Conroy," she mumbled. Earl rubbed his chin. Of course, none of this explained how Kent had so much money in the first place. "Say, did George Kent ever handle money for a bake sale?"

Gloria jolted. "Um, what bake sale?"

"I don't know, maybe Candlewick needed a new tennis court or something."

She shook her head. "No. I never heard a thing about it."

Earl pressed ahead. "It doesn't have to be a bake sale, specifically. It could be any kind of charitable event."

She snorted. "George Kent? I'm sorry—I shouldn't speak ill of the dead. But George was not a giver."

"Would he have had any access to large sums of money? Maybe

he helped with some campaign or had a job somewhere?"

"What do you mean?" Gloria took off her glasses. "What money?"

They were interrupted when the inner door was yanked open. The managing director himself, Ed Nelson, in all his glory, frowned at Earl. "Oh. Are you still here?"

CHAPTER ⛩ EIGHT

Ushering the two into his office, Nelson bent to shake Earl's hand. "I'm Ed Nelson."

Earl gauged the man's handshake. It was firm. "Earl Walker." He nodded to College. "This is Miss Jenny Hutton."

"Sit right there." Nelson motioned to a chair, then he seemed to notice Earl's wheelchair and switched his focus to Jenny. Turning back to Earl, he smiled awkwardly and went around behind the desk.

Earl used the few seconds to take in the surroundings. A futon couch was folded against the wall, its bright throw pillows bringing a splash of brilliance to an otherwise drab room. The wood-paneled walls were adorned with framed certificates and plaques. Earl could not read any of them from his vantage point, but he could not imagine it mattered. None of Nelson's credentials seemed to make a difference when the state inspected Candlewick Retirement Community and decided to shut it down.

Jenny jerked forward in her chair. "Mr. Nelson, we came to complain."

"If this is about the ruling of the state—"

"Actually," Earl cut him off, "we wanted to discuss a matter of some delicacy." He heard an odd clicking and glanced at the fancy clock on the wall. The second hand seemed caught on the minute hand, doing its best to push through and tell the correct time.

Nelson settled in his chair. The man's desk was mostly neat, except for the sandwich leaking on the blotter. There was the greasy smell of corned beef. "So, what can I do for you?"

Earl forced himself not to fidget. "We are here to discuss the incident last night."

Jenny sat forward with a sudden jerk. "How do you come off firing that—"

Earl gripped her arm, and she stopped. He turned to Nelson. "What did the sheriff find?"

The man jerked his head and frowned. "What are you talking about?"

Earl cleared his throat, wondering how dry the air in the office was. "Surely the sheriff came last night. Or sent somebody out."

The man started rocking his chair. "I'm sure I don't know what you mean. Everything was quiet out here last night." Nelson stopped rocking his chair. His weak grin wobbled and disappeared. "Maybe you better state your real business here."

Earl, undeterred, gripped the wheels of his chair and began flexing his fingers. "You have to know—the kid called you. I was there."

"This must be some mistake. You could—" The man stopped. "Wait. How are you involved?"

Jenny sighed and stood. "Maybe we should take our story to someone else. The newspeople, maybe?" She turned to Earl. "Come on, Mr. Walker."

Earl nodded and started to turn his wheelchair.

"Wait." Nelson pressed on the arms of his swivel chair and

pushed himself up. "Please."

Jenny and Earl shared a look. Jenny took her chair again.

"Well." Nelson flashed a tired version of his earlier used-car-salesman smile. Made eye contact with each of them. Took to his fancy swivel chair again. "Now, Mr. . . ."

"Walker. Earl."

"Yes. Mr. Walker. Please tell me your story."

Earl tilted his head. "Last night there was a secret visitor making a racket in Kent's apartment. I was in the hall."

"So you saw someone?"

"Um. . .no. But I heard someone." Earl nodded. "So I went to the front desk, and I found that boy."

Jenny piped in, "Grant Caine."

"Yes," Earl agreed, "Mr. Caine." He sighed and clasped his hands. "I told him what I heard, and he made a call." He looked at Nelson and smiled. "He called you."

Jenny jumped in again. "And somehow that sweet boy got fired!"

Earl grumbled, "Well, I don't know that I would call him 'sweet.' "

"Caine? We had to let him go. I don't know what business it is of yours." Nelson leaned forward, taking a big stapler off his desk. He leaned back in the chair again, clicking the stapler needlessly. "It is management's job to make these decisions."

"But why was he fired?"

Nelson pushed himself up again and walked to the framed certificates and plaques on the wall. He looked at them for a few moments. Without turning around, Nelson spoke. "The state comes down here; they don't know anything. They aren't here for the day to day. They just swoop in and make their snap judgments."

His shoulders slumped, and he turned to the window behind his desk. Out in the common garden, an old woman with clippers pruned a tree. Nelson turned back to Earl and Jenny and let out a deep breath. "Candlewick is having enough trouble. We do not need to file any false police reports."

Nelson sat back down in his chair. He tried to smile. "Besides, I'm sure that you mean well, but this so-called intruder was a figment of your imagination, Mr. . ."

"Walker. Earl." He coughed. "I was there."

The man shrugged. "There was no evidence of a break-in."

"When we got there, the door was open." Earl frowned and looked down, trying to remember. The door was open, right? He looked to Jenny for some sort of reassurance, but she was no help—all she had was his word for it.

"No, Caine opened the door with the key," Nelson said. "As the man on duty last night, he had the passkey in case of emergencies."

Earl pressed ahead but felt his resolution melting. "But. . .the place was a mess."

"I'm afraid that, in his excitement, the young man did that."

"But I heard noises. I found Grant and he called you—then he ran to the apartment. I followed. I got back there not long after him."

Nelson smiled slyly, taking note of the wheelchair. "Seriously. How fast could you have possibly gotten there?"

Jenny leaned forward. "Why, you—"

Earl cut her off. "I know what I saw."

Nelson leaned forward, elbows on the desk, and locked his hands together. He looked at Jenny and flashed the salesman smile. "Miss. . .Hutton. Have you looked into new living arrangements for your grandfather?"

Earl grouched. "She's not my granddaughter!"

Nelson, undeterred, kept his eyes on the young woman. "There are only a matter of days left before he is out on the street. As bad as it is for all of us, the stress is worst of all on the residents. When the mind is under so much pressure, it tends to invent things." He rapped his knuckles on the desk. "Now, if you'll excuse me, I'm very busy."

Earl leaned forward in his wheelchair. He gritted his dentures. "I was a witness. That counts for something."

"But what did you actually witness?" Nelson smiled grimly. "Do you know what it was that you heard? Do you know what it was that you saw?"

"I. . .um. . ." Earl looked at Jenny. She couldn't help. She hadn't been there.

Nelson clapped his hands together. "Well, I can see this was all a big misunderstanding." He stood and went around the desk, leading them to the door. "But I've wasted enough time. I have to ask you to leave."

Jenny huffed. "But what about Grant's job?"

The man grimaced. He stood for a moment then began to straighten his tie. "I have a job to do. And I cannot do my job with a hotheaded kid running in and ransacking residents' apartments and then trying to bring in the authorities unnecessarily."

Earl snorted.

Nelson looked down at him with cold eyes. "There are more than one hundred residents here at Candlewick. There are official procedures to file a grievance. I suggest you follow the rules like everyone else, and we can assess your situation accordingly."

Jenny stuttered, "B–but. . ."

"Come on, College," Earl said in a low, gurgling voice. He

wheeled himself out to the front office. Jenny followed.

"Good day." Behind them Nelson sneered, "My door is always open." The phone on his desk started ringing, and he turned his attention away from them.

Outside the office, Jenny leaned close to Earl. "What are we going to do now?" Her voice was low, quivering.

Earl gripped her elbow and squeezed, tried to give her a consoling smile. "Not much we can do. We tried." He glanced back through the open door. Nelson was pacing as far as the telephone cord would let him, fidgeting with his tie with his free hand.

Jenny was still talking. "Mr. Walker?"

Earl looked at her. "What?"

"He knew more than he was telling. If he's trying to cover this up, do we call the county sheriff ourselves?"

Earl was straining to hear Nelson's side of the phone call. The man was growing increasingly agitated.

"Mr. Walker? Mr. Walker?"

Earl gave Jenny a look and turned his chair back toward the man's office door. Nelson caught sight of him and, with a disgusted look on his face, walked over and slammed the door closed.

Earl grunted, turned his chair, and wheeled himself toward the exit. "Well, there's nothing more we can do here."

"Nothing? But what about Grant?" Jenny's voice betrayed her sharp disappointment.

Earl didn't answer because he was painfully aware that he was again at Gloria's desk. The woman, busily adding folders to a long filing cabinet drawer, pushed the drawer closed. "Well, hello!" She smiled awkwardly at Earl and patted her hair. "So, um, did y'all work your problem out?"

The younger girl got as far as "We didn't even—" before Earl cut her off.

"Mr. Nelson suggested we pursue, um, other avenues of redress."

"Ooh." Gloria gave him a playful smile. "You sound like Matlock!"

"Is that good?"

"Oh, it's adorable." As soon as the words were out of her mouth, Gloria blushed.

Earl pretended he didn't notice. "Well, the experience has helped me understand how little I know about Candlewick. I can't find where anything is around here."

"Oh, that's a shame. It was always such a nice place."

"Say, I have an idea." A smile curved Jenny's lips. "You're familiar with Candlewick—maybe you could show Mr. Walker around."

Earl squirmed. "I'm sure the lady is too busy for—"

Gloria beamed. "I finish my shift at four, if you want to do something after that."

Earl grumbled. "That seems kind of soon for—"

"Sure," Jenny said. "He would be thrilled. Right after your shift?"

Gloria patted her curls. "Well, give me a chance to go home and freshen up. Maybe five o'clock?"

The ladies finished making arrangements, and Jenny and Earl excused themselves. Earl could barely contain himself until he and Jenny reached the hall. "I cannot believe that! I do not need a social secretary."

Jenny, trying to steer Earl's wheelchair back to his home, chuckled. "Apparently you do."

Earl stopped the chair. "We're going the wrong way."

Jenny squinted down the hall. "No, I think this is the way to your apartment. We need to get you ready for your date."

"That's not for a couple of hours yet. Besides, we need to go to Kent's apartment."

"Oh?"

"And it's not a date."

CHAPTER NINE

When they got to Kent's apartment, the front door was wide open. Earl heard a lot of clunking. "Don't they ever lock these doors?"

"Maybe the sheriff came after all," Jenny said. "I bet he's got people inside dusting for prints."

"I don't think so. They wouldn't make so much noise." Earl looked along the rows of doors to apartments. There was no one else in the hall.

He thought about the cranky old man from the night before who threatened to call the police. Had he done it? If the ruckus was enough to make two of the locals come out into the hall, surely others woke up and peeked out their doors. He thought at least one of them would have called to complain.

Earl strained his ears but could not hear any evidence of the other residents. Just the hum of the air-conditioning.

One end of the hall led back to the main complex. The other led to the exit. Sunlight streamed in the glass door. Earl wondered whether a glass door like that was a deterrent to criminals.

Getting to the door of Kent's apartment, they looked inside and stopped. Some of the big furniture was gone—including the couch and the entertainment center. The lamps were wrapped in bubble tape. Boxes were taped up, marked, and ready to be moved.

Earl carefully wheeled his way inside, navigating through the obstacle course. All the framed pictures were stacked together. The plant Earl had "depotted", was browning in the corner, roots exposed. The pile of dirt had been tracked through, revealing big boot prints.

There was noise from the back room, the rumbling of voices and the thumping of boxes being stacked roughly. Jenny whispered, "Mr. Walker, what if we—"

He waved her to silence, sniffing the air. There was the pungent odor of cleansers. "They're trying to cover up the evidence."

She frowned. "The sheriff?"

A fat man came out of the bedroom, huffing and puffing as he pushed a two-wheeler loaded with boxes. He stopped when he saw Earl and Jenny. "Oh." *Huff. Puff.* "Hey."

Earl grunted. "What's all this?"

The burly man, shifting his weight, twitched his unkempt beard. "The dude who lived in here died."

Earl waved the answer away. "Why are you taking away his things?"

"We got orders." The man tilted back the two-wheeler and pushed it forward, trying to circle Earl's wheelchair. All the same, Earl had to scoot out of the man's way.

Two more large men came out carrying the bedroom dresser. They paused when they saw Earl and Jenny, nodded curtly, and got back to their carrying.

After all three were gone, Earl set his jaw. "Come on." He gripped the tops of his wheels firmly and rolled himself through to the kitchenette. All the cabinet doors were wide open, their contents gone, no doubt shoved into the boxes already taped shut.

Earl checked the fridge—it was completely and thoroughly empty. Of course, Earl reminded himself, that had already been the case before.

Closing the fridge door, he turned his attention to the kitchen drawers. They were slightly open, one even crooked. Earl rolled up to it and pulled, but it was stuck. It seemed to be off its track. He yanked harder, and the silverware inside jangled as he jerked the drawer open. Hmm. The movers hadn't packed it up yet. Earl lowered his head and tried to see behind the drawer, but the angle made his head spin. So he stopped.

He tried to push the drawer back but found it difficult. He glanced at Jenny and grunted, "Shut this."

While she took care of the drawer, he went to the bedroom. There was not much left to see—the movers had already emptied most of it. Earl wondered how much longer they had before the movers came back. He glanced at his wrist—he really should get a watch—and decided to just be quick about it.

He checked the closet. It still seemed to have all its contents— shirts, pants, big beige overcoat. Lined up on the floor were all kinds of footwear—slick dress shoes, slippers, galoshes. There was also a box of auto supplies. Jumper cables, jack, mini-shovel. A half-empty plastic jug of anti-freeze had leaked on the carpet.

"What are we looking for?" Jenny was standing in the door. "Look, those men will be back any second. I want to help Grant get his job back, but can't we work on this from somewhere else?"

Earl pointed to the corner. To his relief, the boxes of record albums hadn't been removed yet. "Check those."

"Why? Did Mr. Kent borrow one of your records?"

Earl turned and looked at her. "All these records—and do you see a record player anywhere in the apartment?"

She glanced around and shrugged. "The movers took it."

He shook his head. "There wasn't one here last night."

"It might be under something. I'm always losing my iPod."

He looked at her. Waited. She looked back. Then her eyes widened. "Oh! Record players are big, aren't they?" She looked at the boxes of LPs, then at the half-empty bedroom. "Then why. . . ?"

Earl rolled himself closer to the boxes. Scratched behind his ear then pointed. "Take that one."

"How can you tell? You can't even—"

"It doesn't have any dust on it. The other boxes are filthy."

"Oh." Jenny reached her fingers under the box and lifted. She let out a surprised grunt. "I didn't expect it to be so heavy."

"It's not so bad."

She chuckled. "Maybe you should try it." Then she glanced at his wheelchair and blanched. "Um, that is. . .I didn't. . ."

"Don't worry about it." He turned his chair for the door. "Let's get out of here."

"We're taking it with us?" Jenny frowned, wrinkling her nose. "Can we do that? I mean, won't that be stealing?"

Earl gripped the wheels and turned back. "I thought you wanted to get that young man his job back."

"Well, the manager told us to file a protest. . . ."

"Pfft. The manager." Earl made a face like he wanted to spit. "Did it ever occur to you that this could all be connected to why Candlewick is being closed down? Like maybe management would rather the place go out of business than let something get found out?"

"Um. . ." Jenny bit her lip. "Isn't that a little paranoid?"

"Look around you! We saw a man collapse in front of us—and nobody thought that was worth investigating?"

"They said it was—"

"And then someone breaks into the man's apartment that very same night? You're going to tell me that was a coincidence?"

"Well, maybe you just—"

"And then the manager tries to deny anything happened?"

"Hmm." Jenny shifted her weight again.

"And these movers—how do we know they aren't the same people who were here last night?" Earl thumbed back to the door. "Either way, do you really want to have to explain to them why you're stealing that box of record albums?"

Her eyes went wide. She twitched, as if undecided what to do with the incriminating box in her hands. "Wait, but I—"

Earl wheeled for the door. "Quick! I don't want you to get arrested for theft." He was already to the kitchenette by the time he heard her shriek behind him. He grinned and kept going. In the living room he navigated around the boxes. He checked his watchless wrist again—he really needed to get a watch. "We'd better hurry."

"I'm coming, I'm coming." There was a *clunk* and another shriek and then some kind of *wa-a-a* and then a *whump*. The girl had tripped and fallen.

Earl stopped and turned his chair. "What happened? Did you break the records?"

She sat on the carpet, rubbing her knee. "I'm going to be fine, thank you."

"Well, get going."

"Probably just a bruise, thanks."

In the hall Earl looked both ways. To their left were the glass doors leading outside—likely the way the movers had gone. He pointed back the other direction. "This way."

Jenny had a slight limp. But at least she was carrying the box.

They had almost gotten away clean when there was a shout. "Hey! What've you got there?" It was the fat guy with the two-wheeler.

Earl and Jenny shared a look. Earl shouted, "Go!" He gripped the rims of his wheels and pushed as hard as he could. The hall forked and they took the left. The hall behind them now out of sight, Earl heard the fat man giving chase. The halls shook with the rhythmic pounding of his boots, the air filled with the growing sound of his wheezing.

Earl ignored the fear clawing at his stomach. If the mover should catch them, what would he do? The big man was certainly a bruiser. And his quarry certainly wouldn't be able to outrun him for long—Earl, just an old man in a wheelchair, and Jenny, a young girl carrying a heavy box. Earl had to give her credit—she hadn't simply chucked it. When all was said and done, he hoped it would turn out to be worth the trouble.

They came upon an old man hobbling on his cane. The man shook his fist at Earl and Jenny, shouting, "Lousy beatniks!"

They reached the end of the hall. "I got turned around." The girl was huffing. "Which way do we go now?"

Earl took a second to flex his fingers. They ached. "I don't know."

To their left was a crowd of old people. Milling around. Laughing. Didn't they have someplace to be? To their right was a long straightaway.

If only he knew his way around Candlewick. Even their recent comings and goings had been too jumbled to keep in context. When he was a bus driver, he had one route at a time and he stuck to it. Gloria was supposed to give him a tour of the place, but that was no help now.

Their hunter was no doubt going to be upon them soon. They didn't have time to dawdle. Earl pointed down the right. "That way." He had no idea where it led, but they couldn't sit and wait for the big man to catch them.

Jenny nodded and walked briskly down the way Earl had pointed. It occurred to him that she was pacing herself not to leave him. "You don't have to wait for me."

"Yes I do."

Earl pushed his wheels harder. The hall was long—Earl got some speed up, the wheels on his chair turning faster and faster. That became a problem when a door opened and a woman stepped out of her apartment.

Earl couldn't stop. He grabbed his wheels instinctively, but when he hit the friction, his left hand snapped back. His right hand kept contact a fraction of a second longer, and he lost his balance. He bounced off the wall, and the wheelchair turned over.

"Mr. Walker!" Jenny had dropped the box of record albums and knelt down by Earl's rag doll body on the hall floor. "Are you okay?"

He nodded. Felt more foolish than anything. "Help me back into the chair."

The old woman watched them for a minute and shook her head. "The idea." Then she shuffled away.

Jenny picked up the shawl and set the chair upright. She struggled to help Earl off the floor and back into his chair. He clutched it and used his arms to lift himself up as much as he could.

The angle was awkward. It took a few careful seconds, but they were soon on their way.

But how close was their pursuer now? How much time had they lost? Earl chanced a look back.

"Hey, let's go this way." Jenny had the box again and was nodding toward an offshoot of the hall. It was a room full of people.

Earl flexed his sore fingers. Nodded.

Inside they found a group sitting on a floor mat taking some kind of stretching class. At the front of the room was a woman giving instructions. All the others in the room were following.

Jenny helped Earl wheel to the far back. She snatched the shawl off his knees, set the box down and sat on it, and threw the shawl over her head and shoulders. Then she looked at Earl, jumped up, and helped him out of his wheelchair and into another chair. She pushed the wheelchair against the wall.

Earl in the chair and Jenny on the box pretended to follow the class. They stretched their arms up and over, up and out, pushed this way, pushed that way. All the while stealing glances at the door.

A few minutes passed. When they saw the fat man again, he was walking with Nelson. The two men were speaking in low tones, eyes darting this way and that. Earl turned away, hoping they wouldn't notice him. He glanced at Jenny, her eyes almost covered by the shawl. She had the makings of a spy.

The two of them stayed for the rest of the class. When the group broke up, they waited while the other old folks walked out.

Jenny breathed a sigh of relief and grinned. "I can't believe we got away!"

"We didn't. He stopped chasing us."

"But I saw him—"

"He thought it was important to talk to the boss."

"At least you got your wish. Someone's bound to call the sheriff now."

Earl grunted. "Can you get me out of this chair?"

CHAPTER TEN

Earl and Jenny got back to his apartment without incident. Neither spoke the whole way. Earl noticed Jenny still had a slight limp. She didn't complain once.

For his part, Earl was sore in all kinds of places. His fingers ached, his legs ached, his knees, his left side, his left arm—he was a mess. He was glad to get back home. If this is what happened when he got involved in other people's business, let somebody else take care of it.

Earl just wanted to get back to his TV and his wrestling. So he could watch someone else get battered for a while.

Jenny carried the box the final few feet to the small, round dining room table and dropped it then went to the couch, plopped down, and let out an enormous sigh.

Earl looked out the door one more time then closed it and locked it. The apartment was dark. He rolled his chair backward from the door, slowly, just a few feet. Watching.

You're being paranoid, Earl told himself. *You got home fine.*

He turned on the lamp and put his hands on his wheels once more and was reminded how much his fingers ached. He needed to rest. This was more wear and tear than his body had seen in years. And years.

He looked over at the box of record albums on top of the table. In his present condition, he was momentarily content to just look at them from a few yards away.

"Thank you." His voice cracked. "You're a great sport."

Still collapsed on the couch, still trying to catch her breath, Jenny waved in reply. She looked around the apartment. "By the way, have you found a new place to live yet?"

"One thing at a time." Earl put his hands on his wheels and forced himself to roll toward the table. The box was too tall on the table for him to reach into from the top. He tried to work his fingers in to get at the thin cardboard sleeves but couldn't seem to get one out.

"Wait." Jenny flailed a second then got off the couch. "I'll help." She stumbled over to the table and took a chair. She pulled the end of the box around and delicately pulled at the jackets with her narrow fingers. She got several of them out and handed them to Earl. He gazed at the big square covers. BILLY MAY & HIS ORCHESTRA. LES BAXTER & HIS ORCHESTRA. She pulled some more out and stacked them—PERCY FAITH, FRANK SINATRA, DORIS DAY, and more.

Earl looked at the BILLY MAY record cover front and back and front again. "I don't get it."

"Maybe there's nothing to get. I mean, I know we got all worked up, but maybe the guy was just chasing us because, oh, I don't know, we stole something out of that apartment?"

Earl shook his head slowly. "I don't know what in the world I expected. But I was so sure." He slipped the black vinyl disc out of the cardboard jacket. He flipped on the overhead light and held the record up, letting the light reflect off it.

"What's that?" Jenny pointed down at the floor around Earl's feet.

Earl looked down. There was a folded sheet of paper. "Huh?"

"It dropped out when you got the record out of the, um, cardboard."

He set the vinyl on the table, reached down, and picked up the paper. Unfolding it he found a name, a series of words, and some numbers on it. "Huh."

"What is it?"

"I'm not sure." He set the paper on the table and grabbed the Les Baxter record. There was another folded paper tucked inside. Earl pointed to the pile of records Jenny had stacked on the table. "Look in those."

When they finished, they found that a good four out of every five record jackets included a paper, each one revealing a scribbled name and a jumble of words and numbers. Twenty-eight different sheets in all.

Jenny made a pile, smoothing her hands over it to try and flatten it. "What do they mean?"

Earl stared at the page in his hand. "I don't know." A few of the listed names were familiar, including Anderson and Stanton. Looking at the entry for Anderson, Earl saw that the number next to his name did not seem to be a telephone number. And then there were other combinations of words that did not make sense to Earl at all—Sunday Best? Hello Mudder? Amber's Diamond?

Jenny glanced at the list. "Some of those look like your wrestler names."

"They aren't any wrestlers I ever heard of."

Jenny sat. "You know, this is private information. I think we should just give all of it back."

Earl frowned. "Excuse me? Who came here complaining that her boyfriend lost his job?"

"He is not my boyfriend!" She tucked a curl of hair behind one ear. "Why, did he say anything about me?"

"And then there's the question of the money." As soon as he said it, he winced.

Jenny sat forward. "What money?"

Earl looked away a second. Finally he let out a heavy sigh. "Under the couch."

Jenny looked at him. When he didn't elaborate, she pushed herself up from the chair and went and looked at the couch. Then she looked at him again.

"There's a metal box under there," he said.

Down on one knee, she looked back at him again then reached under the couch. She came back to the table with the metal rectangular box. "What is it?"

"More than fifteen thousand dollars."

Her eyes went wide. "Wow! How long'd it take you to save up that much?"

Earl shook his head. "I found it in Kent's apartment last night."

"You stole something out of his apartment last night, too?"

"Borrowed. There's a difference."

"I'm not sure the sheriff will see it that way."

"At least I'll get a chance to report what happened last night."

"When you confess that you stole that money?"

Earl turned the chair and squinted at her. "When I tell them that something funny is going on around here."

"And why should they believe you?"

"I was there."

She leaned forward and squinted. "Yes, but why should they believe you?"

"I—I. . ." He was taken aback. "What do you mean?"

"Think about it." She waved a hand. "You're just some old man in a wheelchair. At least, that's what they'll say."

He slouched. "Maybe."

"Of course they will. You have no witness, no evidence, no proof."

Earl pointed at her. "We watched that man die!"

"People die all the time. That doesn't mean—"

"What about your friend? He was there last night."

"And he was fired for being a bad employee."

"But I thought you felt—"

"I'm just saying what the police will say. If Grant is a disgruntled employee, why should they listen to him? You're a lonely old man in a wheelchair; why should they listen to you? It's your word against the director's." She held both hands out. "Whose word would *you* take?"

Earl opened his mouth to say something, shut it. Finally he waved a hand toward the table. "There's all the money."

She leaned forward, crossed her legs, put her hands on her top knee. "Which you stole."

"But they couldn't. . ." He stopped. His shoulders sagged again. "They couldn't."

"You know what I think?"

"You've made your thoughts perfectly clear. I'm some doddering old man who can't be trusted to be left alone."

"No—I think we need to pray about this."

He squinted one eye at her. "You really think it's that bad?"

"We don't pray because things are bad. Well, I mean, we pray when things are bad, but we don't pray *just* when things are bad. We pray for guidance."

Earl locked his hands together, leaned forward, and asked in a low voice, "Do you really think *He*"—Earl rolled his eyes up toward the ceiling and then back to her—"cares about this kind of stuff?"

"He cares about all of it, Mr. Walker."

"He didn't seem to care when I got shot in the leg." Earl rubbed his knee.

"He always cares."

"He shows it in a funny way."

"Just because we can't understand everything about God doesn't mean He doesn't understand everything about us. And He does speak to us. But we have to listen." Jenny scooted her chair close. "I'm not saying we have to make a whole production out of it. But we really should take it to the Lord." She waved her other hand at all the stuff on the table—the records, the papers, the cash. "We don't have any idea about any of this—but He knows."

Earl grunted. "I suppose." He shut his eyes and bowed his head. He assumed the girl did likewise, because she started to speak in a low voice. Earl wondered what to do with himself while she prayed. Every time his mind wandered, he had to rein it back in. He thought about the bowling game at the recreation center. About the trip in the hall. About the party. About Kent in the rec center, in the hall, at the party.

Earl sneaked a peek at the girl. Her eyes shut tight, she was still in midprayer. She spoke softly but firmly.

Asking for wisdom. For health. For strength. For her friend Earl. He needed guidance, he needed friends, and he needed a new home.

Earl closed his eyes and bowed his head again. He thought about Gloria. Tried to avoid that topic. He wasn't ready.

He thought about the director, Ed Nelson. The man refused to acknowledge that an intruder had been in Kent's apartment. He refused to call the sheriff. He had something to hide.

Earl opened his eyes and took a wrinkled sheet off the table. A scribbled name, some scribbled words, and a scribbled series of numbers. He looked at the money. "Blackmail."

"—all our needs." Jenny was praying. She stopped and opened one eye. "What?"

"George Kent was a blackmailer."

They both stared at each other. Before Earl could think of the next thing to say, there was an insistent banging on the door. A voice cried, "Open up! Open up!"

Earl and Jenny exchanged glances. Earl said, "The sheriff." He looked at the table. "We've got to put it away. It'll be easier to explain it before they see it."

He grabbed the money, she grabbed the record albums, he stuffed the metal box, she refilled the cardboard box—*bang, bang, bang*—he closed the metal lid best he could, she stuck the notes down the side of the box, he picked up the box of money and looked around, she picked up the box of LPs and looked around—"I demand that you open this door!"—he wheeled for the couch, and she headed for the kitchenette.

There was a rattling of the doorknob. A brief silence, then the jangle of keys. A key in the lock.

Earl frowned and tilted his head. The sheriff had a key to his apartment?

The door slammed open. It was Ed Nelson. "Where is it?"

Earl and Jenny looked at each other. Earl looked back at the man. "Um. . ."

"You took something from Kent's apartment."

"Why would you think I did that?"

"Because the description was 'an old geezer in a wheelchair' "—
he smiled at Earl—"and 'some chick.' " He smiled at Jenny. There
was no friendliness in the expression.

Earl said weakly, "That could be anybody."

"Let's just say I had a hunch." Nelson held out his hand. "Give
it back. It doesn't belong to you."

Earl and Jenny exchanged looks again. Earl wondered what
her God thought he should do now. He turned to Nelson, a
smile creeping across his lips. "Call the sheriff. We could have an
interesting discussion with him."

Nelson hesitated. Then a Grinch-like smile curled his lips.
"You know, I could make life very difficult for you."

Jenny sat up. "Are you threatening him?"

"Who, me? Absolutely not." Nelson raised his eyebrows. "All
I'm pointing out is that life can be dangerous for an invalid. One
simple filing error could result in medication being switched. One
change in a person's menu could bring disastrous consequences."
He narrowed his eyes. "Look what happened to Kent." Nelson's
face went soft again, and he tsk-tsked. "Poor, poor man." He
looked at Earl. "Besides, who's going to take your word over
mine?"

Earl nodded, defeated. "You're right," he grumbled.

Nelson said, "Now give me that box, and I'll be on my way."

Jenny, shoulders slumped, went to the kitchenette and came
back with the box of record albums. She set it down on the dining
room table. "Here."

Nelson saw the corner of a note sticking out, pulled it out,
and looked at the scribbling. An expression almost crossed his
face before he caught himself. He tilted his head toward Earl. "I

bet you have the money, too."

Earl's eyes widened. He opened his mouth, but nothing came out. So he shut it. Turned the chair for the couch, tried to reach down, but found he couldn't. He pointed. "Under there."

Nelson shot a glance at Jenny then sidestepped over to the couch. Got on one knee, always keeping his eyes on Earl and Jenny. Without looking down, he leaned and felt under the couch. He jabbed his hand once, twice, then hit something. He smiled and looked down to drag the metal box out. He opened the lid. "It better all be here."

He snatched the record albums, setting the metal box on top. At the door he stopped. "Mind your own business. You'll be much safer."

CHAPTER ⛫ ELEVEN

Nelson was gone several long minutes before either spoke. Jenny asked, "What are we supposed to do now?"

Earl scratched the side of his nose. "I, for one, would like to find out how he knew about that money. Which, I guess, means I need to call off seeing Gloria." He reached for the phone.

"You'll do no such thing! If you let that man stop your date, then he wins."

"That's crazy talk. We need to plan our next move. And it's not a date."

"There is nothing we can do about any of it right now. And she's going to be here in a few minutes. So you need to get ready."

"My arms are kind of sore after—"

"She can push the wheelchair. Get going."

Jenny waited in the living room while Earl washed up. Despite her insistence, he refused to take a shower. He just wet a washcloth and a bar of soap, washed his face and under his arms.

In the next room she sang some happy tune. Earl stopped with the washcloth and growled. "Stop that!"

"What?"

"That singing!"

"Sorry." She stopped. Temporarily. After a few minutes of songless bliss she started up again.

Earl set down the washcloth again. "Stop that!"

"Sorry," she called out. "I'm just so thrilled you're going out on a date."

"It's not a date." He put the washcloth under the faucet and ran the water.

"Then why are you getting cleaned up?"

"A man can be civilized without folks jumping to conclusions." He began washing out his ears.

"I'm just thrilled that you're finally connecting with your fellow residents. Good for you."

He squeezed out the cloth in the sink. "You make it sound like your pet dog is finally playing nice with the neighbors' pets."

"Sorry! I didn't mean for it to sound like that. It's healthy for you to get out and be with people. And if it's with a lovely lady, all the better."

He came out of the bathroom. "But I'm a married man."

"You're a widower—which means you're free to see other women. Trust me, your late wife is fine with this." Jenny paused. "How long has she been gone?"

"Twenty-two years." Earl was silent a second. Then he rubbed his hands together. "Gotta brush my teeth." He wheeled himself back into the bathroom.

Out in the living room Jenny said, "I think it's time to go back out into the world and make some new friends. We all need people. Like the Bible says. . ."

"Fine, fine, we all need people, amen." He got the brush, the paste then pulled his teeth out of the glass where he had put them to soak. He began brushing vigorously.

"And she can show you around Candlewick." Jenny went into his bedroom and started going through his closet. "Gloria Logan seems to know a lot of people here. She can really help you make a lot of friends."

"Not to mention she can really give me the inside edge." Earl poked his head out of the bathroom. "By the way, can you set the TV recorder? There's a show I want to see."

"Um, okay." Jenny met him in the hall. "What did you mean by that?"

"While I'm out making friends, the TV recorder can—"

"No, the other part. She can give you 'the inside edge'?"

"Yeah. Gloria knows the place; she knows the people. She's the perfect—"

"So, you're going to ask her to help you?"

"I don't think I can very well ask her straight out. It's not really her business."

"So, you're going to take her out under false pretenses."

"Don't blame me." Earl stopped brushing. "You're the one who set this up."

"I don't know about this."

"The instructions for the TV recorder are in that drawer over there."

She was going through his shirts in the closet. "No, I mean— about your going out like this."

He resumed brushing the dentures in his hand. "But you said we had to get that boy his job back."

"You don't have to break that poor woman's heart in the process."

He came into the bedroom, where a shirt and pair of pants were laid out on the bed. The girl was still digging through his closet. He grumbled, "What are you looking for?"

A muffled voice came out. "Where are your ties?"

"I, um. . .don't have much in the way of ties. Why do I need a tie?"

Jenny dug her way back out of the small closet. "So, when you say 'don't have much,' you mean. . . ?"

Earl's eyes flickered back toward the living room. "The dresser drawer."

"A drawer?" Her face fell. "This can't be good."

"Just the shirt will be fine." He reached for it.

"Don't put that on yet. I still have to iron it."

"You don't need to iron it."

"You're not going out on a date in a wrinkled shirt."

"I'm not going out on a date at all. It's more like. . . reconnaissance." He took note of her grunt of disapproval as he wheeled to the closet. He took out a pair of black shoes, a tin of shoe polish and a brush, and got to work. "Think of this as being like secret agent work. There were spies in the Bible, weren't there?"

"Um, sure. But that was different."

"How?"

"I don't know how, but I'm sure it was."

"Uh-huh." Earl sighed. He checked the results of the left shoe. Nice and shiny. He began on the right shoe. "Look, I'm a longtime antisocial hermit. I have a lot of years' practice being a grumpy old man. I don't know how to talk to people."

"Just relax and. . .talk to people."

Earl paused, brush in midair. "I don't know how to do that."

"Talk to them like they're. . .people."

"I don't know how to do that."

"Oh!"

"What?"

"Your ties are wadded up in your sock drawer. Where is your iron?"

"In the closet. I think."

She finally found the iron under the sink behind a bunch of stuff—cleansers and rags and garbage bags. "Now, where is the ironing board?"

"Why would I need an ironing board?"

She held up the iron. "You press this against it. Usually with some sort of cloth in between."

"Try using the cutting board. It should be on the counter."

"Ew. No."

"Well, then I don't know what to tell you."

Jenny sighed. Finally, she made do with a towel on the dining room table.

"This is a bad idea," Earl said. "Maybe I should just cancel."

Jenny breathed in deep, thinking. "It might be safer."

"Safer? Why, what is she going to do?"

"The manager threatened you. That's something to consider. Maybe you shouldn't be out."

"Oh, that. Wait—are you flip-flopping on me?"

"You flip-flopped first."

"Yes, but. . .but. . .well, I don't have an end to this sentence. So, can you set the TV recorder for me or not?"

"I don't know," Jenny said.

"You don't know how to set the TV recorder?"

"No, I don't know if you should still go on this date." She scrunched her nose. "Although I'm not sure how to set this TV recorder either."

"But all along you've been pestering me. There should be a set of instructions in the drawer. And it's not a date."

"I don't think this is the right thing."

"No, that drawer."

She presented him with a black and red–striped tie, a partially ironed blue and white–striped shirt, and an attempt at ironed tan pants. Earl frowned. "Is all this necessary?"

"Trust me. It'll be cute."

He took the clothes and wheeled for the bedroom. "I don't know. Seems mighty fancy for reconnaissance."

"Okay, first of all, this is not reconnaissance. You're going to be in the company of a lady. Second of all, you better believe she's dressing up for this, too."

From behind the closed door Earl asked, "You think so?"

"I know so."

"How can you know?"

"A girl knows these things."

"Maybe I should call it off. Stay home."

"Oh no you're not!"

Several minutes later, Earl opened the door. He was nearly dressed for the evening but still needed help with the tie. "You're the one who says I can't go out with a woman under false pretenses. Besides, if we can't get the TV recorder to work, I've got to watch a wrestling match."

"Stop." Jenny shut the drawer. "Forget the TV. Maybe we should sit back and regroup. What are you afraid of?"

"I'm not afraid." He paused. "Much."

"Look, the battle is half over. She really likes you."

"That's what I'm uncomfortable with."

"It's nice for you to go out with someone your own age—

well, age range—and in the process, you'll get a chance to see Candlewick. It's shameful you've been here all this time and never used the facilities."

"Seems pointless to complain now. What with the state shutting it down and all." He fumbled with his tie. "Can you help me with this?"

Jenny came and pulled up his collar and got to work. "When Candlewick closes down. . .are you going to be able to find a new place that offers all this?"

"I don't want to think about it. You know, I was doing just fine until you pushed me out of the apartment. Since then, I've been accosted, I've witnessed a horrific death, I've been chased, kicked, crashed into a wall, threatened. . . ." He adjusted the tie. "And now I'm going out on a date."

"Ah-ha!" Jenny pointed a triumphant finger. "I knew it was a date!"

"That doesn't mean I have to like it. I'll just try to focus on the job."

"No—no job, just date. Just a nice evening with a nice lady. You can be friends—you can be more than friends—but you will not string that poor lady along. You're going to try being a normal person for once."

"You want to get that kid his job back, right? So, we need to figure out who George Kent was blackmailing."

Jenny wrinkled her nose. "I thought he was blackmailing the manager?"

"With all those notes—not to mention all that cash—Kent must have had several victims. And I'll bet you dollars to donuts they're all here at Candlewick. So one way or the other, there are people in here who know something important."

"I'm getting worried about you."

"About my state of mind?"

"About your safety."

"That's sweet. But can't your God take care of me or something? Maybe send His angels down to protect me or something?"

Jenny sniffled. "Yes, God can do anything. But we're not supposed to deliberately put ourselves in harm's way. Especially if we don't even know what we're doing." Jenny got the brush. "Here, let me check your hair." She wheeled him over by the bathroom sink and the mirror.

Earl fidgeted. "Is all this necessary?"

"Yes. Now stop wiggling." She ran some cold water over the brush then brushed one side of his head. She tilted his head a little. "Where is your razor?"

"Is it that bad?"

"Just a little on the neck here."

"You know, if I hunch down in the chair, she won't even—"

"Razor."

Earl sighed and pointed. "Left drawer."

"When this place closes down, where are you going to go? Who do you even know?" She sprayed the shaving cream into her hand and rubbed it gently on the back of his neck.

"I don't want to think about it."

"But that's the point—you only have a few days left." She scraped the razor across the back of his neck. "So you better think about it. And maybe you better get acquainted with Gloria Logan while you still can."

"What's the point of getting to know people? They always leave."

"I'm here."

"For now. But one day you'll get your class credit or whatever, and it'll be time for you to move on to the next thing."

"That's not. . ." Jenny stopped. "I won't just abandon you."

"But you'll move on. And why wouldn't you? All I'm saying is, everybody leaves. So why bother getting your life all tangled up with other people?"

Jenny sat on the couch quietly for a few moments. Finally she said in a soft voice, "What a sad way to live."

He shrugged. "It's the only way to live."

"Let me check your breath. Ew." Jenny went to her purse on the couch, dug around in it until she found a half roll of Certs. "Here." She held them out then stopped. "Wait—any food allergies?"

"To breath mints?"

"It could happen."

"Well, no breath-mint allergies that I know of. Not that it matters," he grumbled. "It's not a date."

"You still want to have nice breath."

"I brushed my teeth."

"Where are they?"

"I left them in the glass. Can you get them for me?"

CHAPTER TWELVE

Gloria arrived at Earl's apartment right on time. When he opened the door and saw how she was fixed up, he was speechless. Gloria wore a purple dress, golden earrings dangling from her earlobes.

When she saw him, she glowed. "Oh! You're so handsome."

He fidgeted. "Thank you."

There was an awkward silence until Jenny jumped in to the rescue. "Now, you kids have a good time." She patted Earl on the shoulder, murmuring into his ear, "Remember—just act like a normal person."

He didn't respond. He just watched College and Gloria exchange good-byes, and then College waved as she took off. He and Gloria were out in the hall before it occurred to him to mumble, "You look very nice."

"Thank you, Blue Eyes." She tentatively reached for the handles of the wheelchair but stopped herself. "What's the protocol here?"

"I don't know what you mean."

"Do I offer to push the chair, or would that be an insult?"

"Either way is fine." Earl shrugged. "If you're in a hurry and you want to get somewhere fast, you can push. If you don't mind us taking our time, I can wheel it myself and you can just walk alongside."

"A walk would be nice." She smiled at him.

He felt something again in his chest. He hoped he wasn't having a heart attack.

Making their way along the hall, Gloria attempted to make small talk. She asked whether he had any kids or grandkids; he did not. She asked if he had plans after Candlewick closed down; he did not. She asked how he spent his time; he didn't want to admit he spent it all watching game shows and pro wrestling, so he said he read a lot.

"I'm not much of a conversationalist," he grumbled. "I don't know how to talk to people."

"You're doing fine." She squeezed his shoulder and gave him a reassuring smile.

Earl felt a blush work up his face. "I guess."

"I heard how you talked to Mr. Nelson today," Gloria said. "That took a lot of courage—he is such an imposing man."

"For all the good it did me." Earl felt the strain in his weary hands but kept wheeling. "You seem to get along with people. How do you do it?"

"I guess you just relax and talk to them." She added, "Talk to them like. . .people."

Exactly what College had said. Earl didn't reply. Headed for the cafeteria, he almost remembered the way.

"Pardon me for saying," Gloria said sweetly, "but I would think a professional bus driver would be better about directions."

"Well, if we would take a regular circuit around the block a few times, I might be able to figure it out. But these past few days, I've had a lot of geographical information thrown at me in a random order."

They didn't say much else until they reached the cafeteria. Over fruit salad, Gloria asked, "So, you drove a bus a lot of years, huh?"

"Ayup." Earl sipped his iced tea. "Almost twenty-six years."

"Wow, that's a long time. My late husband, Dwight, bless his soul, worked on cars. He died doing what he loved—he was under his favorite Chevy, changing the oil."

"He worked on them? My hat's off to him. I can drive 'em, but I could never figure out how they worked."

"When did your wife Barbara pass away?"

"Twenty-two years ago this spring."

"Was she still with you when. . .um. . ." Gloria glanced at Earl's wheelchair.

"When I was shot by hoodlums and forced into retirement?" Earl sipped his tea. "Yeah. She helped me through it."

Gloria put down her fork and looked at Earl seriously. "What happened?"

Earl paused and took another swig of tea. "So one day, these guys get on the bus. Most times, I paid better attention to potential troublemakers. You have to, for the safety of your passengers and the other people on the road. But I got distracted."

"Why, what happened to make you distracted?"

Earl set the glass down. He stared at the table. "You know, I'm still not comfortable talking about it."

"I didn't mean to pry."

"That's all right." Earl caught himself staring into Gloria's eyes and tried to focus on his real reason for being there. He forced his eyes to wander, take in the people, the place.

She went back to her fruit salad. "So, what do you do now?"

"Oh, the usual." Earl's attention was on the lady behind the counter, her hair in a net, her hands in gloves. "I read. Watch television."

"Actually, I meant for exercise. You don't go outside much at all, do you?"

"Hmm? Oh. Never saw the need." The cafeteria lady was transferring plates of lasagna from her cart to under the heat lamp in the glass case. Earl turned and found Gloria staring at him. He tried a weak smile. "I was just—"

"Do you need me to introduce you? She's married, but she may have a sister."

"Oh. Um. That's okay." Earl began fiddling with his lasagna. Then he leaned across the table. "Listen, do you think she could poison a guy?"

Gloria looked up, alarmed. "Is there something wrong with your food?"

"No, I just—"

"You're not having an allergic reaction, are you?"

"Not that I know of."

"Because a food allergy is serious."

Earl held out his hands. "No, no, no." Gloria was still alarmed; Earl took a deep breath. "I was just asking whether you thought she could poison someone."

"Well, she puts the food out. Did she say something to you?"

"No, everything's fine. Just fine."

"Because if she said something—"

"No. No."

Gloria did not seem completely convinced but went back to her fruit salad.

Earl looked back at the counter. He watched the customers line up, get their trays, pick their entrees off the hot bar, and slide their trays down to the next station. The system was too random for a food handler to target a specific person. It was either poison the whole room or nobody. "Did George Kent have any food allergies?"

Gloria stopped, a forkful of cantaloupe in midair. "How would I know?"

"You work in the office. I thought maybe you would've heard something."

"Why does it matter?"

"If Kent had special dietary needs, he may have had his food prepared separately. Then if someone wanted to poison—"

Gloria slammed down her fork. "I'm going to talk to her."

"No, no, don't—"

But Gloria was already gone. He watched her confront the other woman. As they glanced in his direction, he shrank in his chair and turned away.

At the next table, two men had stopped eating and were staring at him. Earl mocked a friendly greeting. "How ya doin'?"

One of the men, wearing a fishing hat, asked, "Did you say the cafeteria poisoned somebody?"

"No! I was just talking about George Kent." When the two men shared a nervous look, Earl decided to move his chair a little closer. "Say, did you fellas know him?"

"I guess." The man with the fishing hat studied his bowl of stew.

The second man looked bored. "It's a shame anytime someone goes just like that."

Earl pressed his luck. "I understand some folks weren't so broken up."

"You're telling me!" The man started to laugh, but the other man kicked him under the table. The second man caught himself. "But still, it's always best to think well of the dead."

"So, did you know Kent as a friend. . .or, shall we say, as a business associate?"

The man narrowed his eyes. "What's it to you?"

"Listen, I'm not trying to get into your business, but there seems to be a real—"

"Hey Charley, do we gotta sit and listen to this guy?"

The man with the fishing hat looked up and jabbed his spoon at Earl. "Where do you get off asking a lot of personal questions?"

"They weren't personal; I just wanted—"

"Maybe it's best you move on with your business."

"But I'm just having my dinner." Earl turned back to his own table, where he noticed Gloria had returned. "Everything go okay?"

She was unhappy. "We should probably go."

Out in the hall Earl asked, "What's the matter? What happened with—"

"Apparently some people don't appreciate being accused of certain things."

"Oh."

Gloria touched her hair. "At least, that's what she said. I have a feeling I'm going to hear about this at the office."

He grumbled, "I can't believe those guys back there."

"What happened? It looked like some sort of argument."

"I was just asking about Kent and they overreacted."

Gloria regarded him. "Why are you so obsessed?"

Earl stopped wheeling his chair. He couldn't quite look Gloria in the eye. "It's complicated."

"You must have been traumatized to see him collapse like that."

"You could say that." He slowly started pushing his chair forward again. They made their way down the hall.

"It's just a blessing no one else got sicker than they did."

"What do you mean by that? I thought Kent had a stroke or a heart attack."

"A half dozen people got sick at that party."

"Really."

"Think about it," she said. "These folks have a diet of oatmeal and prunes day in and day out; they're not accustomed to alcohol and spicy food. I guess we were just blessed George was the only one who died. Mark had to get dialysis."

"Mark?"

"Mark Conroy. Our host."

Earl nodded. "Tell me about him."

"About Mark?" Gloria paused. "What do you want to know?"

"I don't know. What is he like? What does he do? Would he have hired a hit man to bump off Kent?"

Gloria was aghast. "A hit man?"

"Sorry, just making conversation." Earl tried to laugh it off. "I told you I was bad at it."

"Well, Mark is a huge collector of stamps. He's got maybe a thousand of them, which he's always pulling out and showing us. I'm surprised he didn't bring the books out at the party. But I guess he was preoccupied with staying by the front door."

They were nearing Earl's apartment. Earl was starting to recognize the hallway. "Was the chili really that spicy?"

"That's one reason I had the milk. It neutralizes spicy foods. Of course, since someone died, Ray may be done making chili for a while."

CHAPTER THIRTEEN

Earl went to the drawer and found the number that Conroy had left him. He wasn't sure what he would ask the man. All he knew was that there were all these little things nibbling at the back of his mind, and he was hoping that the host of the party could help him lay some of them to rest.

When Earl called, the first thing the other man asked was whether Earl had seen the ring. Earl said he had not.

"Well, I can't talk long," Conroy said. "I have to head for the general store before it closes."

"Maybe I'll meet you there."

When Earl got to the Candlewick general store, he found Conroy by the canned beets. He grunted, "I'd rather die than eat those."

Conroy looked down at Earl in the wheelchair and smiled. "Some of us can't be so choosy. Folks get to a certain age, they gotta look out for themselves."

"Fun talk from the man who threw a chili party."

The man looked around nervously. "Hey, easy with that talk."

"What's the matter? Are you afraid the nurses will hear?"

"I'm more afraid that too many people will want in the next

one. You saw how crowded my little apartment was. How many more do you think would be able to fit?"

Earl grumbled, "Well, you have room for at least one more."

"Huh? Oh, you mean poor Kent. Yes, that was horrible. I may end up dropping the whole party altogether."

They reached the canned fruit. Earl said, "I heard you had to get dialysis."

"Eh?" Conroy started reading the back of a can of peaches. "I gotta flush the kidneys out three times a week. Luckily I was already scheduled for right after the party." He set the can in the basket. "We were all risking our lives, I guess. It is one thing to have the thrill of the risk, like we're all looking down the chasm. But when one of us actually falls over the side. . ." He let the sentence trail off.

Earl read the back of a jar of artichokes. He set it back on the shelf. "What if Kent was pushed? There is some question about whether he died of natural causes or not."

Conroy jolted. "I don't get you. What are you saying happened?"

"Someone may have done something to Kent. Maybe they even passed something dangerous on to him at the party."

They had reached the cereal. Conroy put a box of granola in his cart, "Why would you think one of my guests killed Kent?" His voice was low, his eyes darting around. "Those are my friends. I've known some of them for years."

"Still, all things being equal, if someone killed him. . ."

"Why think it at all? Did the sheriff find something suspicious?"

"No. Everyone assumed he was just an old man and it was his time to go."

"Well." Conroy went for the next aisle. "Kent was old. We're all old."

Earl followed. "There was something wrong at your party. I saw it." He wrung his hands. "I just can't put my finger on it. Yet."

Conroy blinked. "You sound like you're being paranoid."

While Conroy went through the checkout process, Earl occupied himself with the display of sunglasses by the front. He kept putting on the dark lenses and looking out the store's front window. He would look through the dark lenses then raise the specs, comparing the same view through different lenses.

Conroy had his basket of supplies ready to go. "Wanna come back and talk at the apartment?"

Reaching his apartment, Conroy fumbled with his keys. "Look, I'm still thinking about what you said." He held the door while Earl wheeled himself inside. Once they were in, he shut the door and continued. "If someone came into my home with the intention of harming one of my guests, I'm all for getting that person." He carried the basket of groceries over to the counter. "But what if it was an accident? Maybe he drank something that reacted with his meds."

Earl situated his wheelchair in the same corner as before. "Why would you say that?"

"One of the health newsletters reported a link between grapefruit juice and medication. The juice has an enzyme or creates an enzyme or blocks an enzyme or something." Conroy took a seat on the couch. "Ol' Kent always had juice. He hadn't had a drink since the kidney operation. In fact, he bragged about it."

"Sounds like he bragged about a lot of things."

"Yeah, Kent rubbed a lot of people the wrong way. Even back to when we were kids, he would get into fights about this or that."

"You've known Kent that long?"

"Yeah. We grew up together." Conroy nodded. "As we grew up, Kent grew into a man with. . .appetites."

Earl tilted his head. "How about you?"

"What, my appetites? I have dialysis three times a week. I can't have much of anything."

"At the party you had chili and rum."

"Well, every once in a while you have to live, you know? Some folks jump out of planes. We do this."

"Did you have a grudge against George Kent?"

"Did he rub me the wrong way every once in a while? Sure. Drink?"

Earl waved a hand. "I don't drink."

"Milk or something?"

"Sure, a glass of milk."

Conroy got up and headed for the kitchenette. He called from the kitchen, "I got annoyed with Kent at times. But with a friend like him, you learn to roll with it. I never had any reason to see him come to harm."

"No?"

Conroy returned with two glasses—milk for Earl, iced tea for himself. "Heck, when he needed a kidney, he got it from my own daughter."

"Really? That's really something."

"Yeah, my daughter, Clara, is special." He got quiet. "I don't know what I would do without her and her family."

"That's nice." Earl sipped his milk. "Let's go through the whole evening, the whole chain of events. Who all had access to George Kent?"

Conroy picked a spot in the middle of the couch. "Well, he

was sitting over here, I think."

Earl pointed. "No, he was right over there." Conroy scooted until Earl nodded. "Yeah, there."

"How can you be so sure?"

"Twenty-five years driving a bus, you remember people sitting down."

"Oh. Okay." Conroy, satisfied, looked around the room. "And . . .anyone at the party could have spoken to him or whatever. He was in the center of the room."

Earl rubbed his chin. "Pretty much."

The two men sat, their eyes analyzing the room, reconstructing the party. Finally, Conroy threw up his hands. "This is hopeless. If someone wanted to do in Kent, it could have happened at any point. I mean, this is a closed community. We eat together. We take our medicine together. We work out together. We spend all our free time together. Anyone, anyplace, could have done it. Not to mention we still haven't ruled out natural causes."

Earl regarded the other man. "Fine."

"Say, have you heard about my collection of stamps?"

"Um. . ."

"I have almost a thousand." Conroy went to the shelf and took down a binder. "I have all of them here." He sat down on the couch and opened the binder on his lap. Earl wheeled closer to take a look. Conroy flipped through a few plastic sleeve pages, each holding dozens of stamps.

Earl frowned. "They're all. . .the same."

"Yes."

"You have pages and pages of the exact same stamp."

"Yes."

"They are completely identical."

"That's where you're wrong." Conroy tapped a finger on the top of a plastic sleeve. "Every stamp has a history. Different hopes, dreams. Each stamp represents someone's message. A letter to a loved one. A resume for a job. An application. A paycheck. Each stamp represents a life."

Earl nodded. "Okay." He pursed his lips and nodded again. "I guess if you wanted to poison someone, you could do it with a stamp."

"I guess." Conroy tapped the plastic again. "Of course, these are all used. It would do no good to poison them—there's no reason for anyone to lick them now."

"Just a thought." Earl locked his fingers together. Through the window he saw the trees moving in the wind. "Like you say, Kent could have been poisoned at some other time. But that doesn't help us." He looked again at Conroy. "Look, when you throw a rock in a lake, it sends ripples in all directions. If you want to find the rock, you start with where you saw it drop in."

"But if the rock represents the point in time when someone—"

"I didn't say the analogy was perfect. This is what we know—Kent died at that party."

Conroy shrugged. "Fine."

Earl shrugged back. Held out his hands. "Look, it's all we have."

Conroy sighed. "Well, let's see, who all was at the party? Ray Stanton. Sally Brouwer. George Kent, of course. Gloria. You. Me. That young lady friend of yours."

"She is not 'that young lady friend' of mine."

"Hey, easy. I'm just saying."

"Who else was there? I remember a room full of people."

"Okay." Conroy chuckled. "Dandy Anderson was there. Todd

Dekker. Rick Wilson. Vince Kaiser. Mark Bronleewe. Brandilyn, Creston, Kathryn, Tim, Melanie, Tony, Robert. . ."

"A full house."

"Like I said, we were at capacity."

"Okay. So we have all those people in the apartment at one time. Who had a grudge against George Kent?"

"Swing a cat." Conroy laughed. "Anyone you hit could be a candidate. He was a man with a big, obnoxious personality. You saw him at the bowling tournament. He wasn't even playing, but he shows up and elbows his way in. That's how he was."

"But is that a reason to kill him?"

"I wouldn't think so. But I guess it might be if he pushed someone hard enough. As to who that person would be. . . ?"

"Okay, let's come at this from another direction. Who was within arm's reach of Kent? Everyone who came in was practically orbiting him."

"Any one of them could have stuck him with a needle."

"You mean like a syringe?"

"Lots of folks around Candlewick get shots. Most of us are accustomed to needles."

"But pulling out a big syringe, jabbing the man in the center of the room, in front of all those witnesses? How do you do that without being seen?"

Conroy sipped from his tea and set the glass down. "Sleight of hand?"

"That would be some trick."

"Illusion. It's called an illusion." Conroy grabbed the coaster off the coffee table. "Look—now you see it." He held it clasped in the fingers of his right hand, passed his left hand over it, then separated his hands again. "Now you don't."

"It's in your other hand."

"No it's not."

"I can see it right there."

"Well, I may be rusty."

"That is a terrible trick."

"Well, my hands aren't what they used to be." Conroy flexed his fingers slowly. "But it's the principle of the thing. I mean, those guys playing Vegas can make live animals disappear."

"That's your theory? A Vegas entertainer infiltrated your chili supper to kill the man as a magic trick?"

"You make it sound so crazy. But think about it—an illusion is all based on diversion. You do something to distract the audience from what you're really doing. Now, think about our party—a big room full of people, everybody is talking, jostling, moving around. It only takes a split second."

Earl had nothing to offer. He rubbed his hands together.

Conroy snapped his fingers. "How about some kind of ring? You see in the movies those trick rings with the little needle. It has poison in the tip."

"That's just in the movies."

"It could happen. I mean, you have the small, sharp needle on the ring. You only have to dip it in the poison. When you break the skin, it puts the poison in there."

"Fine. What happens then?"

"Well, at any point in the evening, somebody jabs him with the ring. They slap him on the back; they shake his hand. . . ."

"Wouldn't he feel it?"

"So what if he does?"

"But he's in a room full of people. You shake his hand with your trick ring, he's going to react when you stick him with the needle, right? Everyone would know."

Conroy thought about this a second. "What if you punched him in the arm?"

"Isn't that the same problem? You would still have the problem of being noticed."

"Who would notice?"

"How about the telltale victim saying 'ouch' and falling to the ground?"

"Ah, but if I hit you in the arm and you say 'ouch,' everybody thinks you said 'ouch' because I punched you in the arm. Nobody thinks 'I bet he was hit in the arm by one of those trick poison needle rings.' "

Earl shrugged. "Maybe."

"It's a thing that people do—they hit each other on the arm. And a guy like Kent, he's a bully. He's going to hit too hard, right? To prove how big and strong he is?"

"But we still have a problem. How about if it was Kent's ring—why would he poison himself?"

"Well, he always takes the ring off to show it to people. He always makes a big show of it." Conroy's eyes lit up. "Maybe Kent was planning to kill somebody else with the ring."

"You mean, he brought the murder weapon to the party—he lost track of it—and then someone else used it on him?"

"Yeah."

Earl frowned. The night Kent died, his ring had disappeared off the table. Did the killer steal it to hide the evidence?

CHAPTER FOURTEEN

Earl kept rubbing his eyes. It was like he had not slept at all. The whole night before, he tossed and turned, his head swirling with questions, with stray facts and wild conjectures. For a man accustomed to the quiet life of a hermit, it was a lot of sensory input to deal with.

He also spent the sleepless night worrying that his "not-a-date" with Gloria had been more fun than he cared to admit, even to himself. She was a charming woman, she was delightful, she was a ray of sunshine. And her interest in him was not entirely unwelcome. But something about her nagged at the back of Earl's mind. Something he was afraid to face.

When the alarm went off, he went several bouts with the snooze button. But eventually he realized he couldn't put the day off any longer. He finally crawled wearily out of bed, took the railing hand over hand around to the kitchenette, and started the coffee.

While he waited for the water to boil, he went around the apartment and turned on the lamps, opened the curtains, switched on the TV. Anything to generate more light in the place. Anything to help him crawl out of this fog.

His mind didn't begin to clear until he finally had some coffee. He liked it thick, black, and syrupy. As it coursed through his system, he was able to dig through the clutter that was his morning brain and decide that the next person on his checklist should be Ray Stanton. After all, Stanton made the chili at the fateful party. He seemed to know the deceased. He was part of that circle of friends. Whether or not he was directly responsible for George Kent's death, he was probably in a position to have seen something important.

Earl checked the clock. It was going on seven. Starting to feel lazy, he went for the phone—and realized he didn't have any idea how to call the man. So he called up the front desk at Candlewick. A voice answered, far too cheery for this time of morning. It turned out to be an answering machine. Earl hung up.

On the end table was Gloria's phone number. She was friends with these people; maybe she knew how to get in touch with Ray Stanton. But Earl wondered whether calling her this morning would send the wrong message. He didn't want to give out inappropriate signals.

So he went about his morning routine—cereal, milk, vitamins, meds, the whole bit. The entire time, the urge to call Gloria became stronger. Earl wanted to hear her voice again.

He put off calling her as long as he could. He brushed his teeth. Brushed his hair. Picked out a shirt, pants, socks. But once he was dressed and ready to go, he was all out of stalling tactics.

She picked up on the first ring. "Hello?"

"Hi." He hesitated. "This is, um, Earl Walker." He was already starting to feel like a punk kid.

"Well, good morning, Blue Eyes," she said. "How are you?"

"Still trying to get my day started, I guess. You sound awfully chipper." Earl wished he had written down some notes before he got on the phone.

"I guess I'm just a morning person. Did you have breakfast yet?"

"I had some cereal."

"Oh."

"With milk."

"Uh-huh."

"Say. . ."

"Yes?"

Earl felt like he was floundering, so he jumped right to the point. "As you've figured out, I just don't know my way around here at Candlewick."

"Yeah." There was a twinkle in her voice.

"So, I was wondering if you could play tour guide for me again today."

"Well, I have to cover the office during the lunch hour. . . ."

"Actually, I was thinking of this morning. Maybe we could swing by and visit Ray Stanton."

Gloria sounded genuinely puzzled. "Ray? Why him?"

"Oh, I don't know. He's just one of the few people I know around here."

"Well, most mornings he works out at the Wellness Center."

"What is that, some kind of laboratory?"

"It's the gym. You know, exercise and stuff. They have weights, they have a sauna, they have—"

"Oh. Sure. Do you ever go to the gym?"

"Why, you want to go this morning?"

Earl's limbs said *No way*, but his mouth said, "No time like the present."

"Well. . ." There was a pause on the other end of the line. "I was planning to go to chapel. I like to go to their Wednesday morning service."

"So, what time is that?"

"It's at 10:00 a.m."

Earl squinted at the clock. "It's not even eight yet. Maybe we could do both?"

"Oh." There was another pause. "If you want to come to chapel, I would like that very much."

Ooh. Earl had blurted out that "we" part. He didn't mean to volunteer for chapel. But he couldn't think of a polite way to back out now. Besides, it was important to get to the gym before Ray Stanton was gone—and he needed Gloria's help. "Sure. That would be fine."

"I'll come by and get you in ten minutes?"

"Fine." After he got off the phone, Earl remembered that he didn't own any sort of gym supplies whatsoever—no clothes, no equipment, no nothing. So while he waited for Gloria to come by the apartment and pick him up, he had to improvise. He more or less picked out his rattiest clothes and put them on for his workout. He then took what he had been wearing before, wadded it up, and stuffed the change of clothes in a plastic bag, adding assorted toiletries he grabbed off the bathroom sink.

When Earl and Gloria got to the Wellness Center, Stanton wasn't there. Earl tried to hide his disappointment. Fortunately his natural grumpiness covered it quite well.

Even after he was resigned to the fact that he might actually have to exercise, it still took Earl some time to find something he was willing to do. The man on duty patiently explained all the options, but Earl shot pretty much everything down. He didn't want to work the balance beams. He didn't want to go in the swimming pool. He had no intention of lifting weights.

Finally, Earl decided on the rowing machine. Which—as the orderly tried to explain—was not as easy as it looked, especially for a man in a wheelchair. In fact, Earl flailed at it awhile.

"Whew!" Earl said between deep breaths, working the oars. It was not fun. "I guess I'm out of practice."

"You're doing great," Gloria encouraged from the nearby stationary bicycle. "We don't have to stay. We can leave anytime you want."

"No, it's fine," Earl said, although the tone of his voice made it clear that it was not, in fact, fine. "I'm still just trying to get my sea legs. So to speak." He glanced over at Gloria on the cycle, pedaling away.

Barbara always liked riding bicycles. On weekends Earl would throw their bikes in the back of their pickup truck, and they'd drive out to the country to find a good stretch of bike trails. Earl missed that.

"Are you okay?" Gloria gave Earl a concerned look.

"I'm fine." Row, row, row. "Say, what can you tell me about Ray Stanton?"

"You want to talk about Ray now?"

"I'm just trying to make up for lost time." Row, row, take a deep breath, row. "I've lived here all this time, and I don't know anybody."

"Okay. Um, lessee. . .well, Ray was a writer for a lot of years. I guess he still does that."

"What does he write?"

"I guess he's a magazine writer."

"Yes, but what kind of magazines? Puzzle magazines, true

crime, romance fiction—"

"Oh! He's a travel writer."

"So. . ."— row, row, take a deep breath, row—". . .he goes on a lot of trips?"

"Not really." Gloria paused, must have realized her pace was off, and pedaled to get back in rhythm. "In fact, I don't know of any time that Ray ever went anywhere. At least, not since he's lived here."

"And how long has that been?"

"Several years, at least."

But if Stanton doesn't go anywhere, how can he be a travel writer? Earl tried to ask the question aloud but found the words did not come out. In fact, it was getting hard to do something as elementary as breathing.

Gloria looked at him again. "Are you sure you're okay? Your face is all red."

"Maybe I do need a break." Earl let go of the oars. He tried to scramble out of the thing on his own but couldn't quite make it.

The man on duty came to assist him. Earl started to grumble that he didn't need the help, but he had a sudden mental image of flailing around on the floor in front of Gloria and kept his mouth shut.

As Earl was deposited on a bench, he saw Stanton enter. Earl was still gasping for breath, so his greeting was more ebullient than intended. "Hey, man!"

Stanton grinned, until he apparently realized he didn't actually know the man speaking. "Good morning."

Earl offered his hand. "I'm Earl Walker. I was at the chili party."

The man relaxed and shook hands. "Ray Stanton."

Earl waved toward the exercise room. "You work out here a lot?"

"I suppose so. You're never too old to stay in shape."

"Especially if you're going to put a lot of poison in your body."

Stanton frowned. "What do you mean?"

Earl glanced in Gloria's direction. Confident that she was out of earshot, he said, "The chili. It was your recipe the other night, right?"

"Yeah. It's a family recipe from way back."

"What all's in it?"

"Sorry." Stanton laughed. "It's a secret."

"But you made an adjustment to the recipe at the party. Is that right? Isn't that what happened to Kent?"

The other man narrowed his eyes. "Exactly what are you saying?"

"I think I'm speaking pretty plain. You made the chili. George Kent dropped dead. What happened—were you afraid that Kent would make your secret public?"

Stanton's eyes widened. "What did he tell you?"

Earl was shooting blind. "Well, for one, you're a travel writer who is afraid to travel."

Stanton started dabbing his towel against his forehead. "That is a filthy lie. I do not have hodophobia."

"Is that what it's called?" Earl smiled grimly. "I find it curious a man would know such a fancy word for an affliction he claims not to have. And I suppose if it got back to your editors that you didn't actually go to any of the places you were writing about. . ."

"You have a lot of nerve talking like that." Stanton shook a fist, but the bravado drained from him. Pale, he sat on the bench next to Earl. "Look, I'm sorry that some folks got sick. We're a bunch of old people whose constitutions can't take spicy food. We were all taking a risk. You were there—you're as guilty as anybody."

"I didn't eat any of the chili."

"Then you're a hypocrite."

"Now wait a—"

"You show up at the party, you pretend to be one of us—and now you want to make a lot of trouble," Stanton said. "Okay, so a few people at the party got sick. Listen, every time we do one of our parties somebody gets sick. They got sick the last time we did it, and the time before that. It's part of the deal. Poor Mark Conroy has to schedule the party around his dialysis. And it's not just my spicy chili—it's also the rum."

"But Kent didn't drink any rum," Earl said. "He had the grape juice. So I think he must have gotten a little something extra in his chili. Now, you were in the kitchen. You could easily have dropped something in his bowl."

Stanton threw up his hands in exasperation. "But why would I even do something like that? Tell me."

"I saw how the two of you were around each other. You hated the man."

"Everybody did. To know him was to hate him."

"Ah, but maybe he was going to tell people about your— what did you call it? Hodophobia? That would have ruined your career."

Stanton dabbed his forehead again. "I am a respected journalist."

"Uh-huh."

"Look, Kent lived hard, he rode hard, and maybe he even died hard. But even if somebody did do something to speed that process along—and let me be the first person to shake his or her hand—there are a lot of people who could have done that."

"But you were the one in the kitchen. You made the chili."

"Sure, I had access to everyone's bowl at the front end. I dished the chili out of the pot into the individual bowls, and then I put the bowls on the counter. From that point, my job was done. Listen, Sally Brouwer was the one who actually served everybody. I didn't even see the bowls after they left the kitchen."

"Sally Brouwer, huh?" Earl tilted his head, scratching the side of his nose.

"And Sally had way more reason than me to kill Kent."

"Why? What reason could she have?"

"Listen," Stanton said in a low, conspiratorial manner. "Sally has a problem picking up things."

Earl squinted. "You mean she has arthritis?"

"No," Stanton replied. "I mean she has kleptomania."

CHAPTER ## FIFTEEN

E arl grumbled the whole way to chapel.

"Come on," Gloria urged. "It'll be fun."

"I don't know," Earl said. "I'm not the religious type."

"That's between you and God," Gloria said. She added, a twinkle in her eye, "Not that I won't do what I can and try to help tip the scales."

She said it in a good-natured way, but it still made Earl uncomfortable. He was also uncomfortable with how things were turning out. The more time he spent with Gloria, the more he found himself wanting to spend time with Gloria. He wondered what his late Barbara would have thought about that. (He wondered what Gloria's late husband would have thought, for that matter.)

The service at chapel was smaller than Earl expected. Just a few people. Four, in fact, including Gloria and him. Five if you counted the person leading the service. The place smelled of lilacs.

He asked, "Do you mind if we stick closer to the back?"

"Normally I like to sit close to the front," Gloria said. "But you're the guest."

In the last row, Gloria moved the chair on the end to make a place for Earl's wheelchair. She sat in the chair next to him.

Earl looked around the small room. Four rows of chairs, some banners on the bare white walls. Up front, a small glass table with a wooden podium on top of it. Smooth music emanated from small speakers mounted on the side walls. To Earl's ears, it sounded like a flute accompanied by acoustic guitar.

"Not much of a crowd," Earl said. "I thought more people went to church."

"This is just a chapel service."

"What's the difference?"

"Every weekday morning, someone comes in to share a little devotional."

"Is that like a sermon?"

"Eh." Gloria pursed her lips, nodding her head from side to side. "In a way. But usually shorter, more of a thought for the day."

"So it's not religious."

Before she could come up with a whole reply, the speaker got up to start. While he read something from the Bible, Earl's attention wandered.

Barbara had been the churchgoer. She had joined the committees, she had gone to the Sunday school parties, and she had attended the special events.

Barbara had never been pushy about Earl going with her. He sometimes accompanied her on Sunday mornings—afterward she wanted to stay and chat with people, maybe even go to lunch with them. He just wanted to get home.

It hurt to think about it. If he had known he was going to lose her so soon, he would have done a lot of things differently.

"What did you think?" Gloria's voice snapped Earl back to the present.

"What?" He shook off his reverie. "Um, fine. It was fine." He hoped there wasn't going to be a quiz.

"I have to go to the office soon. Did you want to get something to eat?"

—

When they got to the cafeteria, Earl was relieved to see someone different handling the food. Looking at his options under the glass, he found it hard to choose. Everything smelled so good. In the end, Earl got the special—meat loaf—and Gloria got a salad. "When do you have to be at work?"

"About an hour. The receptionist has her lunch at twelve thirty."

Earl tried to be polite. "So, do you work there a lot?"

"A few hours here and there. I cover for the regular receptionist for her lunch and also when she needs to be out of the office for something."

"I guess it's pretty handy to live in the same building where you work."

"Yes, it's pretty nice." They ate in silence, focusing on their food a few seconds. Then, looking Earl in the eyes, Gloria asked, "So what did you really think?"

Earl stopped chewing. "Think?"

"About the chapel service."

He chewed a little more while he struggled to come up with an answer. Finally he had chewed all he could and swallowed. "It was fine."

"What were you thinking about?"

"Just now?"

"During chapel."

Ouch. He thought he had been more discreet than that. He

took his fork and knife and cut up some more of his meat loaf into smaller pieces. "I was thinking about how Barbara used to drag me to church."

"She was a Christian?"

"Yes."

"How about you?"

Earl cut his meat loaf into even smaller pieces. He wondered how long he could do that before he broke it up into its original ingredients. "I guess you could say that God and I are not exactly on speaking terms."

"You're never too old to start."

Earl put the fork and knife on the table. "He's already taken everything that matters to me. I don't have anything left to give."

"It's not like that. The world is what takes it from us. The Lord wants to help us through it."

Earl grunted. "Well, He hasn't exactly been doing a bang-up job."

"You can't blame God for your losing your wife. When she died, He was sad, too. Besides, you're still here. You're still alive."

Earl pushed back his plate. "I guess I better get back home."

"Oh." Gloria couldn't hide her disappointment. "Of course." She started gathering up their dishes. "I'll help you get back to your apartment."

"I can make it."

She stopped. "Are you sure?"

"Gotta learn sometime." He gripped the top of the wheel rims, his hands still sore, and turned for the exit. He paused and swiveled back. He couldn't bring himself to make eye contact. "Thank you. For things."

"Will I see you later?"

Earl hesitated. Then he nodded once. "I guess." He got as far as the door before he stopped. He couldn't just leave like this. He waited until Gloria finished returning the dishes and throwing away the trash.

When she saw him waiting, a hopeful glow curled across her face. "Forget something?"

"Where do I find Sally Brouwer?"

Her smile disappeared.

—

Earl followed the shaky directions—Gloria didn't ask why he wanted them, and Earl didn't volunteer any explanation—and ended up at Sally Brouwer's apartment. He waited until a few residents passed. He didn't want to give any untoward impressions. Then he wheeled up to the door and reached for the buzzer. He couldn't quite reach it, so he rapped his knuckles on the door.

There was the sound of rustling inside. A muffled voice called out, "Just a minute!"

Earl cast a worried glance each direction. Fortunately, all the other residents down this hallway were apparently out living rich, full lives. Bowling. Volleyball. Hang gliding.

The door opened and there was Sally Brouwer, her long black hair pulled back into a ponytail. She looked at him uncertainly. "Are you here to sign the petition?"

"Um." Earl looked at her blankly. "No."

"Oh." She closed the door.

Earl stared at the closed door for a second, then rapped his knuckles across it again. There was the sound of rustling, then a muffled voice, "Coming!" The door opened. Sally gave him the exact same look as before.

Earl showed her his dentures. "Did I say no? I meant yes."

Sally grinned and stepped back, opening the door wider. "Why didn't you say so? Come on in!"

She disappeared into the apartment. Earl hesitated then wheeled inside. He didn't get far before he ran into a pile of papers. He looked around the apartment, goggling at the stacks and stacks of papers. They were stacked on the couch, stacked on an end table, stacked on a coffee table, on a chair, in the breakfast nook. . .everywhere.

His hostess returned from somewhere and handed him a sheet of paper and a pen. "Wait, I'll find you something to write on." She got a hardcover book and handed it to him. "There."

Earl looked at the paper. "Do you mind if I read this first?"

"It's all very basic, really. We just want the return of Bob Barker."

"From *The Price Is Right*?"

"Exactly."

"But he did the show for some thirty years. He retired."

"Right. So this is a petition to demand that Bob Barker return as host of *The Price Is Right*. Just sign on the line there."

"I. . .see." Earl looked down at the paper. He did promise. He signed his name, never more glad he had so few friends at Candlewick Retirement Community. The idea of having his name attached to this was bad enough, but at least almost nobody would recognize it.

Hand still shaking, he handed the paper back to Sally. "Here." His voice cracked. "Good luck." It was all he could think to say.

"Thank you!" She took the sheet and went to a stack by the lamp. She counted down from the top, lifted the top stack, and slipped in the petition about a third of the way down.

"So. . .saving up for a paper drive?"

"No." She looked puzzled. "Why would you say that?"

"No reason. I just happened to notice all the papers. You know."

"Oh. These are all petitions."

"These are all signed?"

"They're works in progress." Sally went to the stack by the lamp. "Like this one here is a petition for the Judds to come perform here."

"Here. . .at Candlewick?"

"Yes."

"Where do you expect them to play?"

"I don't know, maybe the lobby."

"And how did you expect to convince Mama Judd to come out of retirement?"

"I hadn't thought of that." Sally bit her lip. "But we can worry about that after we have the petition finished."

"How many signatures do you need for something like that?" Earl didn't have the heart to ask where one would send it.

"We have five so far."

"I see." Earl leaned over the coffee table and snatched up a handful of sheets. There were petitions regarding all manner of things: how the coffee should be served in the Candlewick cafeteria, that the TV network should air more "quality programs in the vein of *Murder She Wrote* and *Little House on the Prairie*," that cats should be allowed to compete in dog shows, that dictionaries should have fewer words in them, that Tide brand detergent should go back to an earlier package design. . . .

"What is this?" Earl squinted at the sheet in his hand, a petition to block the television networks from using modern technology to create brand-new episodes of *Perry Mason* using computer-generated images of the late Raymond Burr. It even had a few signatures on it.

Sally nodded. "They can do anything with computers now."

"But who in the world do you send a petition like this to?"

She shrugged. "We'll worry about that after we get enough signatures."

Earl spread the stack out on his lap. "How many copies do you make of each petition?"

"Sixty or seventy. Sometimes a hundred, if it's popular."

Earl looked at the stacks around the apartment. "How can you afford so many copies? These must have cost you a fortune."

"We get free copies in the computer room. When the machine works."

"Maybe you broke it making too many copies."

"Not usually. In fact, Saturday was the first time I couldn't get my copies."

"Wait—Saturday? I thought you were at the bowling thing. Then I saw you at the party."

"I was trying to make my copies before that. I have a life, you know. Besides, Saturday mornings are the best time to make a lot of copies without anyone complaining about somebody using up all the paper."

Earl wondered whether he had just gotten to the bottom of the question about why the printer wasn't working when he and Jenny were there.

As his eyes adjusted to the clutter, he also began to notice odds and ends scattered around the crowded apartment. Trinkets. Baubles. "You have a regular antique show there."

"Maybe." Something about the question seemed to make her

nervous. "What about it?"

"Did you ever find out what happened to George Kent's ring?"

"His ring? Why would you ask that?"

"Because you came looking for it," Earl said carefully. "And then I got to thinking how earlier that day, Kent was showing his ring around. When he noticed you, he made a special point to. . . well, protect it. In fact, his special point seemed to be that he was afraid you might take it."

"That's crazy. You don't know what you're talking about." Sally seemed agitated. She made a show of shuffling her various petitions, as if it was suddenly very important that she refile them in different orders. If there was a system to it, Earl couldn't tell what it was. "I'm very busy now."

"I can see that." Earl tilted his head. "You were serving people at the party."

"There were several of us serving." She dropped her armload onto the couch and gathered up another set of papers. "I think."

"But you served the beverages, right?"

"I may have. . .no, wait—George didn't want the rum. You should remember; you both turned it down."

"But you still served the chili. You could have poisoned him."

Sally dropped her papers on the end table. "Poison? But George died of a stroke or something."

"Actually, it was kidney failure. Maybe because of something you dropped in his bowl of chili."

She pushed aside some papers and sat on the couch. She breathed heavily for a few moments. "Someone really poisoned him?"

"Maybe."

She looked at him with indignation. "And you think I did it?

Dandy was there, too. He was in and out of the kitchen."

"But there was no love lost between you and Kent. In fact, I heard you were relieved when he died."

"That's a horrible thing to say!"

"Is it? I apologize for being rude."

"Besides," she said, lip trembling, "Dandy was the one who owed George so much money."

Earl remembered the "double or nothing" bet between the men at the bowling tournament. "Yeah, I guess he lost some amount of money Saturday."

"Oh, that's not the half of it. Dandy lost money to George all the time. All. The. Time."

Earl found his way back to his apartment. Without Gloria's help it took some doing. A memory of their last conversation flickered. He tried to put it out of his mind.

When he finally got to his apartment, he called the front desk. "How can I reach a Mr. Dandy Anderson?"

"We're really not allowed to give out the numbers."

"Well, can you transfer me to his number?"

"Hold, please."

The phone rang, but no one picked up. When it finally went to voice mail, Earl panicked and hung up. Then he consulted his scraps of paper and found Conroy's number. That one got through, and a familiar voice said, "Hello?"

"Hi, this is Earl Walker."

"Oh. Of course." He was tentative. "Listen, I'm meeting family in a few minutes, so I can't really talk right—"

"I was looking for Dandy Anderson."

"Well, he's not here."

"I was wondering if you happened to know where I could find him?"

"This time of day, some of the fellas are in the rec center. He could be there. In fact, that's where I'm meeting my family. Why don't you come out?"

"Maybe I'll do that." There was a knock at Earl's door. He said into the phone, "There's someone at the door. I guess I'll see you around."

"See you at the rec center?"

"Sure." Earl hung up and went for the door, where he found Jenny waiting. "Hello, College," he grunted, "Are you coming here every day now?"

"I just came to see how you were doing."

"I'm fine." He hoped his grumbly voice would warn her to stay clear. "So you can be on your merry way."

"I also wanted to talk to you." She looked down the hall. She seemed nervous.

"If this is about Gloria, I don't want to—"

"It's about that poor Mr. Kent."

"What now?"

"I know how he was murdered."

CHAPTER SIXTEEN

Earl looked out in the hall to make sure no one was watching. "You better come in and sit down. I'd hate for you to pass out before you had a chance to share your wisdom."

Jenny made a beeline for the couch. "By the way, have you found a new place to live yet?"

Earl held up a hand. "One thing at a time. You were going to tell me about a murder. . . ?"

"Oh—it was so simple! You're going to kick yourself when you hear this." She glanced back at the man in the wheelchair, eyes widening. "I'm sorry. I—I. . ."

Earl motioned for her to sit. "Just tell me. I can see you're about to explode."

"Well." Jenny put her hands on her knees and took a second to collect herself. "You know how we were in the recreation center on Saturday afternoon, right? There was the bowling tournament, and there was, I think, a shuffleboard or something, and there was the billiards table. . . ."

"A room full of people leading rich, active lives." Earl rubbed his hands. Would the soreness ever go away? "Where are you going with this?"

"That's where George Kent was murdered."

"But we saw him later, at the party."

Jenny clapped her hands together. "Look, I know that was where we saw him, er. . ." She paused.

Earl looked at her. "Collapse?"

"Um, yes," she said, relieved to have gotten past the indelicacy. "I know that we saw. . .that. . .happen at the party. But the murder actually took place earlier that day. In the recreation center."

"Far be it from me to point out the implausibility of your theory," Earl grumbled. "But there was a room full of witnesses. Somebody would have seen something."

"And that would be different from your own theory, how?"

Earl set his jaw. "Go on."

"It was the playing cards." Jenny, glowing, paused to let the declaration sink in.

Earl squinted. "You're not serious?"

"Yes!" Jenny pantomimed the card game. "You deal a hand of cards. Is that what you call it? A hand? Anyway, the cards are razor sharp. George Kent gets a paper cut, the card has been poisoned, and the poison goes right into his blood."

Earl locked his fingers together. "And you're saying that's why he keeled over at the party?"

"He went right to the party after that. The poison had enough time to course through his system. . . ."

"Without everyone else at the card table being cut and poisoned, too?"

"Not all the cards were poisoned. Just the ones the dealer gives to Mr. Kent."

"And how does the dealer not cut himself on the deadly playing cards?"

"I don't know. Maybe he wears gloves."

Earl looked at her doubtfully. "I see."

"It explains everything."

Earl folded his hands. "Of course, you're ignoring the central problem. George Kent didn't even stop at the card table."

"But. . ."

"We saw him when he came in. He walked around the room once, he stopped at the billiard table, then he came to where we were at the, um, bowling tournament."

"Huh." Jenny's shoulders slumped, and she slid back on the couch. "It was so simple."

"Sorry to pop your bubble there."

"Wait." Her eyes lit up, and she sat forward again. "You just said it."

"I did?"

"It was the chalk."

"The chalk? We're talking about chalk now?"

"Like you said, he stopped at the billiard table. They have chalk, right?"

"I guess."

"The victim chalks up his cue or puts the chalk on his hands. He does something with the chalk."

"And it's been poisoned?"

She pointed, grinning. "Exactly! The chalk has been poisoned, and it gets into his skin or his pores or something like that. Or maybe he breathes it." Jenny looked at him expectantly.

Earl took in a deep breath and let it out. He gripped the wheels on his chair and headed for the kitchen. "You want something to drink? Water? Juice?"

"No thank you. So, what do you think?"

Earl got a glass and pulled the grapefruit juice out of the fridge. He made a point of calculating how much time had passed since he took his meds.

He heard Jenny's anxious voice from the other room. "Mr. Walker?"

Earl took his juice back to the living room. He smiled at her then took a swig. It was cold and bracing. He swallowed then let out a satisfied sigh.

Her expectant face whittled to disappointment. "You don't think it was the chalk either, do you?"

Earl looked at her with pity. "All those other people at the table, all using the chalk. And the idea it was an airborne poison? That's like a biological weapon or something. You would have poisoned the entire room."

"Oh." She was deflated. "Dumb, huh?"

"Unless"—Earl scratched the side of his nose—"the killer did poison the entire room."

Jenny frowned. "You think so? But we were all there."

"What if Kent was allergic to something? I heard about someone who dropped dead on an airplane because someone else opened a bag of peanuts."

"Really?"

"He was so severely allergic that just the peanut dust in the air killed him."

"Wow."

"Wait." Earl shook his head. "No, no, no. That's crazy."

They sat in silence. Finally Jenny said, "We should still go to the rec center and investigate."

"Investigate what? The random allergies? The chalk? The cards?"

She shrugged. "All of it."

"Absolutely not. We'll look like idiots."

"What would be the harm?" She looked at him. "I mean, we could at least go to the recreation center and look around, couldn't we?"

Earl mumbled, "Maybe I can find Anderson there."

Jenny leaned forward. "What was that?"

"The recreation center, huh? Well, let's go!"

He got to the door and outside before Jenny got up from the couch. "Hey," she called after him, "wait up!"

Already out in the common garden, Earl smiled to himself. But despite the cramps in his hands, he kept going. After all, Jenny had two good legs. She could no doubt catch up.

The sun in his face, Earl squinted as he smelled the honeysuckle. It still made him think of Barbara.

And then he thought of the way he had treated Gloria. He was ashamed. But he was too embarrassed to think how to make it right.

Earl almost made it straight to the recreation center. Only one wrong turn along the way. The recreation center was as enormous as he remembered. Light burst through huge windows, casting shadows across the dark red carpet. The big room was rollicking. Those residents not relaxing in comfy chairs chatting or watching television were engaged in one of several activities, from darts to cards to billiards to board games.

Jenny was almost jumpy with enthusiasm. "So, do we start with the billiard table or what?"

Earl, searching the faces in the room, turned and frowned at her. "Huh?"

She motioned with her hand. "Or should we start with the

cards? If it was the cards, do you think they would still be here somewhere?"

"It wasn't the cards."

"I'm just saying, as long as we're here. . ."

"It's not the cards."

"Well, what about the billiards then?"

"What about them?"

"Do we start with the sticks? Or do we find the rosin cube? Is that what you call the chalk? Rosin?"

"Um. . ." Earl was half listening, still trying to find his man. "What?"

"Do we sneak the chalk out; do we need the sticks—"

"What are you talking about?"

Jenny leaned in and spoke in a low voice. "I don't think they're going to let us conduct forensic tests here on-site. So we need to get what evidence we can and take it to some remote location for—"

"I wasn't aware we were qualified to conduct forensic tests at all."

"Well, I was talking about having the professionals—"

"Fine." Earl saw Dandy Anderson hanging out by the dart game at the far wall. Glancing back at Jenny, Earl said in a conspiratorial manner, "Listen, I think your best bet is to check the eight ball. It might have a bomb in it."

She wrinkled her nose. "You're kidding, right?"

Earl wheeled himself across the room. He passed a card table where they seemed to be playing Go Fish. He chuckled to himself and kept going.

Reaching his destination, he found a huddle of men gathered around a line made on the carpet by a crooked piece of duct tape. Earl recognized two of them: Mark Conroy and Dandy Anderson.

Conroy noticed Earl and grinned. "Hey, man, you came back."

"I guess so."

Conroy turned to Anderson. "This is Carl—"

"Earl."

"Earl, from the bowling tournament. Remember?"

Anderson nodded at Earl. "Oh, sure. Here for a game of darts?"

Earl waved a hand. "No, I don't think so. I'm surprised they let you have such sharp objects in the room like that."

"These?" Conroy held up one of the darts to reveal its flat Velcro tip. "The worst they can do is stick to your suede shoes."

"Well, anyway," Earl said, "I'd have to stand for that, wouldn't I?"

Anderson leaned in. "You don't have to throw the darts to play along, if you know what I mean?"

Earl said, "I don't think I—"

"He's not betting with you, Dandy," Conroy cut in. He turned to Earl. "His leg medicine makes him gamble."

Anderson huffed, "But—"

"Besides," Conroy asked the man, "aren't you in the hole enough already?"

"My luck is going to turn around. You'll see." Anderson turned to Earl, as if his opinion mattered. "You'll see."

Earl felt awkward. He had hoped to catch Anderson alone, but now it seemed like this was his only opening. "Maybe we could discuss this," Earl said. "Privately."

Anderson and Conroy exchanged a look. Conroy shrugged and went back to the game, where the others were waiting for him to take his turn.

Earl wheeled a few feet away. He stopped in front of the big glass doors to the outside.

Anderson followed, doing his little trademark dance shuffle the whole way. When they were ready to talk, he was practically drooling. "So, how much you thinking? Twenty bucks? A hundred?"

"I'm thinking about fifteen thousand, two hundred dollars."

Anderson jolted. His eyes almost popped out of his head. "W–what? You really want to gamble for so much money?"

"Not really. But I thought it was the sort of numbers you liked to play." Earl nodded at the man's legs. "So, you used to be some kind of dancer?"

"Still am." Anderson crossed his legs and spun around, ending with a bow. "You're looking at the 1969 regional champion."

"Really. And that would be the regional champion of. . . ?"

"Absolutely. The call will come any day now."

Earl squinted. "The call from who?"

"Hollywood, m'boy, Hollywood." Anderson tipped an invisible hat. "They're always on the lookout for professional dancers. I just have to keep in shape and listen for that ol' telephone."

Earl was flabbergasted. Did any of these people listen to themselves? He hoped he wasn't as delusional. He said, for lack of any better idea of a response, "I guess that's why you take the medicine."

"Yep. Gotta keep the legs strong and stable."

"Even though it has such bizarre side effects."

Anderson hesitated. "Well, you take the good with the bad."

"Tell me, how bad is it?"

"How bad is what?"

"Your gambling problem. When Kent died, did it wipe your slate clean?"

Anderson narrowed his eyes. Licked his lips. They were trembling. "What business is it of yours?"

"You were with Kent at the party before he collapsed. You gave him the cigar."

"No I didn't. He must have had it with him."

"Well, then you lit it."

"I did not!" Anderson's face got soft and puffy, like he was near tears. "I didn't. I tried, but I couldn't." He wiped an eye. "I wasn't the only one who owed him money. You don't know what you're poking into."

"Tell me." Earl set his jaw. "What am I poking into?"

"You don't know." The man was wiping both eyes now. "I've got a problem. I'm not responsible."

Earl nervously looked around the room. The card players were breaking up. The billiard players were setting up another game. At the dart game, Conroy was joined by a woman and a small boy. Was Anderson going to make a scene in front of all these people?

"Once we're all scattered," Anderson was blubbering now, "the whole operation will be gone."

"Wait." Earl snapped back to attention. "What did you say?"

"Well, we'll all be gone then, won't we?" Anderson's voice was stronger now. "Then it'll all be over."

"Go back a second." Earl was sure he'd missed something. "What did you—"

"Well, gentlemen," a voice interrupted them, "you missed your chance." Conroy had approached them, a woman and child in tow. "The game's over. Nothing left to bet on, I'm afraid."

Earl and Anderson exchanged a look. Earl said, "Just as well, I guess. I don't have a lot of money to throw around." He looked at the young woman with Conroy then at the small boy. He tried to think of something friendly to say. All he could come up with was "Hello."

The boy hid behind the woman's leg.

Conroy said, "This is my daughter, Clara Johnson."

She offered a hand to Earl. "How do you do?"

Earl smiled and shook her hand. "So you're the one who donated the kidney?"

She gave him a funny look. "Yes. Yes I did."

"Your father mentioned it. That was a brave thing that you did."

"Thank you."

Conroy added, "And that young'un there is my grandson, Marky."

Earl waved at the boy, who continued to hide behind his mother. The grown-ups laughed.

Conroy bent down for the boy. "Hey, what's that behind your ear?" Conroy's eyes opened wide—an expression matched by the expectant child's—as he displayed empty palms. Then he quickly snapped a hand toward the boy's ear and brought out a shiny quarter. "Did you lose this?"

"Yeah, Gampa!" The boy eagerly snatched the coin with tiny fingers.

Conroy chuckled and tousled the boy's hair. He looked up at his daughter. "Why don't you all head on over to the cafeteria. I'll catch up." They exchanged a kiss and she and the boy took off. Then Conroy said, "Hey, Dandy, can I speak to Carl—"

"Earl."

"—Earl here, alone a second?"

Anderson looked at Conroy uncertainly, then he gave Earl a wicked look and left them.

"Whew," Conroy said, taking the handles on the back of Earl's chair. "I don't know what you said to him, but he was not happy."

"He's not the most stable man I've met. But he did say something very strange about some kind of 'operation.' Would you happen to know what—"

"Listen." Conroy maneuvered Earl by the far wall. "I just wanted to speak to you privately. Dandy is a very emotional person."

"I can see that."

"Don't take any of what he says personally. The medicine he takes for his legs really does a number on his personality. Gloria was saying how nervous you get around new people—"

"I can handle myself. Wait—Gloria said what?"

"Nothing bad. She just said—" Conroy glanced toward the entrance, then dove for Earl. "Look out!"

He tackled Earl hard and the chair turned over, the two men tumbling by the wall. There was a loud *chok* in the wall.

"W–what happened?" His head spinning, Earl glanced toward the entrance of the recreation center. From this vantage point, it was a giant tilted angle. A crowd was formed, looking curiously at the two old men embracing on the floor.

"Someone just tried to kill you." Conroy reached over and pulled something out of the wall. It was a big knife.

"Are you all right? What happened?" Jenny had run up to them, frightened.

Conroy pointed to the exit. "Someone threw a knife at us!"

She nodded and ran after the phantom. Earl called out to her, but he couldn't stop her. He grumbled, "She's going to get hurt."

"I'll help her," Conroy said. "You going to be okay?"

Earl nodded. Conroy darted for the exit. Leaning on one elbow, Earl looked at the big knife lying on the floor, then he squinted at the exit. Someone had thrown that knife across the room, and it had lodged in that wall right behind him.

It was a room full of people. It could have been a stupid prank. It could have been meant for someone else. It could have been a coincidence.

Earl wasn't buying any of that.

CHAPTER ⫟⫟ ⫟⫟⫟ SEVENTEEN

An elderly man looked down at Earl. "Are you all right?"

"How do you think I am?" Earl tried to prop himself up on an elbow. He flailed, feeling for all the world like a turtle on its back.

"Do you need a pencil to bite on?"

Earl gave the man a look. "Now why would I need that?"

"When you have a seizure, you're supposed to—"

"I am not having a seizure!" Earl flailed harder, hoping the man would take the hint and help him up. "Someone just tried to kill me! You were right here; didn't you see it?"

The man shook his head. "I can get the nurse if you want."

"Can't you just help me up into that chair there. . . ?"

"But that's a wheelchair."

Earl grunted. "I was pushed out of it when someone threw a knife at me."

"If you're hallucinating, I should probably get you a nurse." The man left him.

"No! Wait!" Earl reached out, but the man had disappeared into the crowd. There was a massive huddle of people blocking his vision. All standing there, shuffling in place, looking at him, afraid to get involved with the man they assumed was having a seizure. Earl reached out his hand. "Could someone please help me back into my wheelchair?"

Nobody moved. Grunting, Earl rocked himself until he managed to flip onto his stomach. He dragged himself toward his overturned wheelchair, one big wheel in the air.

He finally got a grip on the chair, tried to figure out how to get it upright and how to get himself into it from the floor. He was not exactly well practiced in this particular act.

Finally someone in the huddle came forward. "Here, let me help with that." The woman grabbed the chair and tipped it back upright. She leaned forward and gripped Earl by his armpits. Aside from his being ticklish, he was also mortified at the thought of a woman rescuing him. He was relieved when the woman called over a couple of men, who came and helped lift Earl and deposit him in the chair.

"There," the woman said. "Feeling better?" She inspected him for some head injury.

"I was not having a seizure!" Earl wiped a hand across his forehead.

"No one said you did."

"Well, that other man, he. . ." Earl let it drop. He looked over at the huddle at the door. Some still watching, others starting to leave. He was a little surprised to notice that, even as they drifted back to their activities—their jigsaw puzzles and their crossword books and their cards and their billiards—they were still between him and the exit. He called out, "Did anyone see anything?" A few looked at him, but nobody answered.

Earl looked at the big glass doors in front of him and then back at the big doorway into the complex. The entire room was between him and the exit. The would-be killer had to have been an excellent knife thrower to successfully throw it through a room full of bustling people and find its way to the wall.

Earl turned to the woman. "Did you happen to see it?"

"Well, we didn't see you until after you fell. If you need a witness for a lawsuit—"

"No, no, no—someone threw a knife across the room. Did you see him?"

The woman looked at him doubtfully. "I thought you said you had a seizure."

"No, I did not have a seizure!" Earl pointed at the man standing there. "You had to have seen it. Either it was thrown from all the way over there—at the risk of some bystander walking into it—or the knife thrower had to come right into the middle of the room."

The man and the woman exchanged looks. The man shrugged. The woman said, "There are a lot of people here all the time."

"I would think he would be kind of conspicuous." Earl stopped. "I'd think the big knife he brought in with him might have been a big giveaway."

"Is this it?" Another man walked up, holding the knife in his hands.

Earl growled, "What are you doing? Don't touch it!"

The man's eyes went wide, and he quickly handed it off to the second man. The second man panicked and handed it off to the woman.

Earl goggled. "No, no, no! You've gotten your hands all—"

"I'll fix it!" The first man snatched the knife back from the woman and, using his shirttail, wiped the handle clean. He handed it to Earl. "Good as new."

Earl was unable to reply.

Just as the three split up and went back to their business, Jenny and Conroy returned. Jenny came and hugged Earl. "Are you okay?"

Earl grunted. "Just need to collect myself." He looked at Conroy. "I take it you didn't catch him?"

Conroy was still trying to catch his breath. "No, he got away clean." He pointed at the knife in Earl's hands. "I shouldn't have pulled it out of the wall like that, but I was so shocked. Maybe there are still—"

"Trust me, there are no prints on this knife." He looked at Jenny. "You didn't see anybody either?"

She shook her head. "What do you think happened? Could it have been some sort of prank?"

Earl shook his head. "No. That was no prank."

"But where could he have gone?"

Conroy nodded, thinking. "Whoever it was didn't wait around. He would have gone to the nearest exit."

Jenny said, "He could have hidden somewhere." She nodded at Earl. "Like we did."

Conroy's ears perked up. "Like you did? When? What did you do?"

Earl waved it off. "Never mind that now."

Conroy said, "Earl, you've been asking a lot of questions these past few days. Pushing a lot of people around. This is a closed community—everyone talks."

"You're saying this was because I was being nosy? Seems kind of extreme."

"Not for someone trying to hide a secret."

"All the same, it's not like I'm the sheriff or anything."

"But," Jenny said, "maybe someone was afraid you would find something and then go to the sheriff."

"It isn't even necessarily someone you talked to," Conroy added. "Like I said, everyone here talks. It could be that you talked to someone, and they talked to someone else about it, and that second person. . ."

"So, you're saying that it could be anyone at Candlewick." Earl waved a hand around the room. "It could be anyone in this room now."

Conroy and Jenny looked around. Conroy nodded. "Scary as it seems, yes. It could. You need to be careful. Maybe even drop this whole thing."

Earl frowned. "What I don't get is why nobody saw anything."

"Maybe everyone was busy. All he had to do was walk by, throw the knife, and keep going."

"Even one of your Vegas entertainers wouldn't be able to make that kind of shot. Look at the distance."

"But an expert knife thrower. . ."

"Then add the ridiculousness of it being an expert knife thrower who tried to kill me. I am hardly a threat to the Vegas entertainment industry."

"Um. . .well, when you put it that way."

"No, whoever it was had to have come to at least the middle of the room. Had to have passed right by people to come in, had to have run past them again to get out. If he left at all."

"So you really think he's still here somewhere nearby?"

"He has to be."

"Then we better get you out of here."

As they wheeled him through the hall, Earl nervously took

stock of every person they passed. He watched for any sudden movements. *You're getting paranoid, Earl,* he told himself. *Then what was that knife back there? Did you imagine that?*

Jenny said, "Do you want to call anybody?"

Earl asked, "Who do you suggest?"

"I don't know. Emergency people."

"Seems to me that the emergency has passed."

Conroy said, "Any family we should call?"

"No." Earl did not elaborate.

Jenny whispered, "He doesn't have any family."

Conroy said, "I'm sorry to hear that. I don't know what I would do without my family." Then he stopped. "Oh, sorry. I didn't mean to sound like I was rubbing it in."

Earl waved it away. "What do you know about George Kent's family?"

"I don't think he had any. I mean, we were friends all the way back to when we were kids. As far as I know, he doesn't have anybody."

They reached Earl's apartment. "Well, I guess I'm home now." He held out a hand to Conroy. "Thanks for your help."

After Conroy went away, Jenny helped Earl into his apartment. They weren't there long before there was an insistent pounding on the door. It was Gloria.

"Oh! Blue eyes, are you okay?"

"Um. Yes."

"Did you call the doctor yet?"

"Where did you come from? I thought you were working."

"As soon as I heard about your seizure—"

"It was not a seizure!"

Suddenly a woman and a man, both in white, appeared at the

door. "Is the patient in here?"

Earl growled, "I'm fine! Go away!"

"Sir, if you had a seizure, we need to—"

Earl tried to regain his composure "Look. My friend and I were in the recreation room. He got kind of excited and knocked my chair over. That's all."

Jenny started, "But, Mr. Walker—"

Earl cut her off. "I did not have any kind of medical emergency."

The nurse looked at him doubtfully. "Well. . ."

"I promise."

"All right then. But you really should have waited until we got there."

"I apologize. Since there was no emergency, it never occurred to me there would be any excitement. The next time I do not have an emergency, I'll be sure to loiter until someone asks whether or not I am dying. Does that sound fair?"

The man frowned. "Huh?"

"You don't have to be rude, sir," the woman said. "We just have your health in mind. Be sure to let us know if you do have any trouble."

"Of course." After they were gone, Earl closed the door.

Jenny tore into him. "How could you not tell them about the killer?"

Gloria's eyes widened like dinner plates. "What? Who was killed?"

Jenny said, "Someone just threw a knife at Mr. Walker! It plunged into the wall right next to him!"

Gloria, horrified, reached out to Earl. "That's so terrible! But who?"

Earl waved a hand. "Stop. Too much information. Stop."

The women both were silent.

Earl wheeled himself farther into the apartment. The women each took a seat, Jenny on the couch, Gloria in the chair next to it. He looked at Gloria. "I'm glad you came."

Gloria's face lit up. "Oh, that's—"

"I need to ask you a few things about Kent."

Gloria deflated. "Oh."

"Everyone hated him. Right?"

Gloria frowned. Looked at Jenny then back at Earl. "That's the question? I mean, I hate to speak ill of the dead, but it's hardly a secret he gave everybody a hard time. He was a pushy man."

"But they hung around him. Gave him money."

Gloria thought for a second then nodded slowly. "Now that you mention it, I guess I saw it every once in a while. Someone handing him a few dollars. But I thought he was just a bully taking their lunch money."

"Hey!" Jenny sat up suddenly. "They were buying him off! He knew their secrets!"

Gloria looked at her uncertainly. "W–what?" She looked at Earl. "What are you saying?"

Earl put his fingers together in a steeple. "I've been working at a disadvantage. I'm the outsider. But you know the people. You know Candlewick."

"O–okay. . ."

"You might also have an idea who would have secrets around here. Whoever tore up Kent's apartment was looking for whatever incriminating evidence he had on them. They had to find it before the sheriff showed up—or before his family came and took all his stuff away."

Jenny said, "But the sheriff never came. And Kent doesn't have any family."

"Yes. But the burglar didn't know that. As it was, the movers almost beat us to it." Earl scratched the side of his nose. "Of course, Nelson was the one who stopped your boy Caine from calling the sheriff."

Jenny said, "And since Kent didn't have any family, there was no one to raise any serious questions about his death."

Earl said, "And Nelson was the one who called the movers, too."

Gloria watched the back-and-forth between the other two like it was a verbal tennis match. "What questions about whose death? What are y'all talking about?"

Earl looked at her. "Hasn't anyone come to the office asking about Kent?"

"Well, I'm not there all the time, but now that you mention it, one or two people may have come in. They wanted to know about his estate. I told them that Mr. Nelson was handling George Kent's will."

Earl narrowed his eyes at Gloria. "They were asking about his possessions or about his money?"

She thought for a second. "I think his money."

Jenny frowned. "So they wanted to try and get their money back?"

Earl sat back in his wheelchair, thinking. The two women watched in silence, occasionally trading glances between them. Earl scratched his nose and finally smiled. "I know why Kent had all that money."

CHAPTER EIGHTEEN

I need to speak to you, Nelson." Earl did his best to show a face of strength. It helped that Jenny, Gloria, and Mark Conroy were with him. "Now."

They had found the managing director in the back part of the outer office, feeding sheets of paper into a shredder. He stopped. Glaring at Earl's entourage, the man locked his eyes on Gloria. "Ms. Logan, what is the meaning of this?"

Gloria put a hand on Earl's shoulder. She cleared her throat. "This gentleman has some very important information regarding the deceased."

Nelson raised an eyebrow, a smirk creeping across his face. "The 'deceased'?"

"Yes sir. George Kent." She nodded at Earl, who was sitting resolute in his wheelchair. "Earl—Mr. Walker—has information that needs to be brought to your attention immediately."

Nelson waved the papers in his hand. "I'm busy. I can't have people barging in and out of here all day."

Earl grunted. "You may be surprised to hear an attempt was just made on my life." He regarded Nelson, narrowing his eyes. "That is, if you are surprised at all."

"Another delusion, Mr. Walker? Perhaps you should consider professional help. We can direct you to some excellent facilities that can—"

"We were all there!" Jenny looked around at their group. "Well, I was there. And Mr. Conroy was there."

Conroy nodded. "Yep. I was."

Earl grumbled, "The hole in the wall in the rec room is hardly my imagination. I'm sure it will be of interest to the sheriff. And once he gets here, I may have some other interesting evidence to share—but you know all about that."

Nelson's smirk wavered then fell altogether. He turned to the shredder and then back to the group in front of him, undecided. Finally he turned for his private office. "Fine. Maybe Mr. Walker and I can speak in here. Privately."

Nelson went into his office. Earl thought for a second then said in a low voice to Jenny, "After we go in, grab as much of those shredded files as you can." He snatched a random sheet of paper off the nearby receptionist's desk and folded it, slipping it under his afghan.

He wheeled himself into Nelson's private office. The other man came back to the door, gave a dark look at the others, and closed the door.

As Nelson made his way around his desk, Earl glanced around the room. The man had been packing up: All the frames were off the walls and stacked in a box. Papers were stuffed into another box.

The stack of papers Nelson was holding before—the ones he had been in the process of shredding—were now on the desk. Earl tried to get a better look, but Nelson snatched them up, sticking them under his desk blotter. He sat behind the desk. "Now, what is this all about?"

Earl folded his hands, choosing his words. "When a man dies under questionable circumstances right before my eyes, I take an interest. But when management tries to perpetrate some sort of cover-up, that just does it."

Nelson snorted. "If you're not careful, you'll be talking to our lawyer."

"Fine with me." Earl tilted his head. "Maybe he can explain how Kent got away with running a gambling operation with impunity here at Candlewick Retirement Community."

Nelson's mouth opened, but nothing came out. He straightened his tie. Finally he sputtered, "Why would you say that?"

"At first I thought Kent had been a blackmailer. Which, of course, would have offered an excellent motive for his murder."

"If he, in fact, was murdered. Which he was not." Nelson inhaled and exhaled deeply through his nose, his tight cobalt eyes locked on Earl.

Earl paused, a tiny smile curving his lips. "But his secret notes were just a jumble of numbers and code words. If Kent was blackmailing these people, there would have been a different kind of evidence—photographs, diary entries, stolen letters, things like that. Something more incriminating than a series of numbers."

Nelson straightened his tie again. He said nothing.

Earl continued, "No, these were too complicated to be coded blackmail notes. But as I thought about it, they did suggest something else."

Nelson asked in a soft voice, "That being?"

"Gambling receipts."

Nelson swallowed hard. His lips moved, but no words came out. At last he got up and went to a bar in the corner of the office and poured something for himself. His hands trembling, he barely got the liquid into the tumbler. "I'm not sure where you get that. I mean, Kent was not really loved by the other residents here. Why would they trust him with their money like that?"

"From what I hear, he was quite a bully. He no doubt bullied many into gambling on his betting operation, whether they wanted to or not."

"But earlier you said it was blackmail." Nelson returned to his desk. He began cracking his knuckles, one at a time. "Maybe the numbers were some sort of code. Hidden messages that told all sorts of explicit secrets." *Crack*. "It's just a matter of finding out the code, and you'd have all sorts of evidence." *Crack*.

Earl gurgled a low, dark laugh. "Seems like an awful lot of trouble. So much coding, so much decoding."

"Okay, so maybe the numbers were some sort of combination for a safe. Or an address to a locked box, like in a bus terminal. Yes, the incriminating materials you mention may have been safely locked away somewhere." *Crack*. "That is, if there were even those sorts of numbers as you describe. This is all, of course, conjecture."

"But these were pages and pages of numbers—how many safes do you think Kent had? No, it makes much more sense that these numbers represented his gambling operation." Earl tilted his head. "But why am I telling you this? You already know all about it. He was a bookie—and you were his partner."

Nelson flashed angry eyes. "You'd better watch who you tell your lies to."

Earl pressed on, undaunted. "You were the one in Kent's apartment that night. You were searching for those receipts."

"Absolutely not!"

"Of course you were. You gave yourself away." Earl nodded a

head toward the frames packed for the move. "When you came to my apartment, you knew exactly what was missing—those hidden receipts." He pulled the folded paper out from under his afghan. He had no idea what was on it, but that didn't stop him from bluffing. "Of course you missed one. Not to mention all those pages you were just shredding. These should be enough to start an investigation."

"Hey!" Nelson jumped up from his chair and snatched the page from Earl's hand. He started to read it. "Wait, this isn't one of the. . ." He looked back at Earl, his face a mixture of confusion and anger.

"Oh, that's not one of the gambling receipts you were trying to shred—that's just something I grabbed off the desk out there." Earl let a smile creep up on his lips. "Gotcha."

Nelson blinked. His mouth moved to form words, but nothing came out.

"When that boy called you," Earl continued, "you were inside the apartment. You knew he was coming. You panicked and ran out before he got there."

"Anybody could have heard him coming."

Earl shook his head. "There was exactly one exit—the apartment's front door. But you left behind the box of money, which meant you were scared away and left in a hurry. The only way you could know that kid was coming was because he called ahead. He called you."

"Someone else could have scared the intruder off—maybe the neighbors."

"The neighbors didn't get involved until after I got there—after you got the phone call and ran away. You left without finding those receipts, so the next day you called the movers to get everything out of the apartment."

Nelson cleared his throat. "That is common procedure when remodeling the apartment for the next tenant."

"Candlewick is going to be closed in ten days. Do you really think someone is going to come rent an apartment ten days before the place shuts down?"

"We're still under appeal," Nelson whined. "Besides, if I were here, why did I have to run away? I work here. I would have had a perfectly good reason to be here on the premises."

"But that isn't what you told the kid on the phone, is it? You said you were at home. If you suddenly showed up after the call, it would have broken your alibi." Earl chuckled. "It's like driving the big bus—when you factor in all the other cars on the road around you, there's really just one place the bus can be at any given time. No other combination will work."

Nelson frowned. "Okay, you lost me there."

"Fine, try this—the movers came and got everything out—at your orders—because you still needed to find those gambling receipts before anyone from Kent's family showed up. With everything moved out, you could leisurely search the empty apartment. And if the receipts turned out to be hidden inside some piece of furniture, you could take your time checking those, too. You could be in the warehouse with the couch or the lamp or whatever for all the time you needed." Earl paused. "But I found the receipts first."

Nelson moved his lips again. His shoulders sagged as he thought for a second. Finally he opened one of the big drawers in his desk. He pulled out a box of cigars, offering one to Earl, who declined. "Suit yourself," the man said, lighting the cigar. He puffed on it a few times then sat back in his chair. This time he leaned far back and propped his feet upon the desk. "How did you find them so easily?"

"You could say that for once my chair was an advantage. If I wasn't trying to roll my way around the end table, I would never have run into the box of money. As for the record albums, when you're closer to the ground, you notice dust. Or, in this case, the lack of it."

Nelson laughed. He puffed a few times then blew a smoke ring. "Forgive me if I don't congratulate you."

"Of course, this looks pretty bad for you."

Nelson meticulously blew another smoke ring. "You'll have a dickens of a time proving anything to the authorities. You're just a crazy old man who got it in his head that this crazy story would somehow save his home. It doesn't make sense how it was supposed to help, of course, but being a crazy old man, you wouldn't understand that."

"I think the authorities will take murder more seriously than that. If there's any—"

"Murder?" Nelson yanked his feet off the desk and sat up suddenly. He pointed his cigar at Earl. "Now you really are crazy."

"You and Kent were running some illegal operation through Candlewick. When the state mandated that the place shut down, all your gambling clients would be scattered to the four winds. One or both of you panicked. It became convenient for you to—"

"That's an awful lot to suppose."

"You could have easily killed him. As you yourself told me when you threatened me—"

He pointed the cigar again. "I did not threaten you."

"Maybe not in so many words. . ."

"Not in any words at all."

"There are a lot of ways a man in your position could kill someone. You'd have all kinds of opportunities."

"Exactly. I'd never be so clumsy. Kent would have died in his sleep."

"When did you try and kill me in the recreation center?"

"Now you're pathetic." Nelson puffed on his cigar. "If I were passing by the window, a dozen or more people would recognize me. How stupid do you think I am?" He puffed again on his cigar.

"I don't know. How stupid are you? You gave Kent those cigars right before he died. They might have been poisoned."

"No." The man puffed again. "You can't poison a cigar with ethylene glycol."

"We'll let the experts be the judge of that." Earl jolted. "Wait—what?"

Nelson puffed on his cigar again, allowing himself a grin. "Didn't have it all figured out after all, did you?"

Earl rubbed his chin. "He was poisoned by antifreeze?"

Nelson went to a box on the credenza. He dug through it until he found a specific folder, which he handed to Earl. "Look at the file yourself. As if it's any business of yours." The man went and looked out the window at the common garden area.

Earl stared at the manila folder a second, then he opened it and tried to make sense of the papers inside. There were a lot of little details—the date George Kent came to Candlewick; his food allergies (corn, milk, egg, wheat, sugar); his birthday in May; his kidney transplant a few months ago.

And right there, in black and white: cause of death, kidney failure.

Earl looked up from the page. "But this just says he died of kidney failure. Where do you get that he was poisoned with antifreeze?"

Nelson looked back from the window. "You didn't really know George Kent, did you?"

"I don't see what that has to do—"

He shook his head. "I cannot imagine anyone who actually knew the man going to this much trouble on his behalf."

"That's a horrible thing to say."

Nelson pointed his cigar. "Kent was belligerent. He really knew how to push your buttons. But, as much as folks may have wanted to kill him, the irony is that he saved them the trouble. It was probably his one act of human kindness."

Earl squinted. "You're saying it was suicide?"

Nelson stabbed his cigar out in the ashtray on his desk. "You were in his apartment. Did you happen to go through his closet?"

"Sure, but—"

"All those auto supplies?"

"Sure."

"Kent hadn't had a car for years. But that antifreeze container was half empty."

"You're suggesting he drank it?"

"Kent was all alone in the world. No family. Except for some long-lost child out there somewhere. With Candlewick closing down, Kent was just too depressed to go on."

"Long-lost child? Who was that?"

"Do you understand the definition of 'long-lost'?"

CHAPTER ▌▌▐▌▌ NINETEEN

Nelson didn't bother to show him out.

As Earl, Jenny, and Gloria made their way down the corridor, the ladies burst out with questions.

"What happened in there?"

"What did he say?"

"And then what did you say?"

Earl refused to discuss anything. "Not out here." He glanced around, suspicious of everyone in the hall. What was that man doing with the walker? Where was that woman rolling that oxygen tank?

They went to Gloria's apartment. The women waited until they got Earl settled. Earl's wheelchair was parked next to the couch. Jenny took the big chair. Gloria went to get everyone some iced tea.

While waiting for the tea, Jenny stared at Earl. He tried to ignore her, taking a few minutes to look around the apartment. If it wasn't for their young chaperone, Earl would never have allowed himself to be alone with Gloria. It wouldn't look right.

Gloria's apartment was—what was the word?—cute. It had the same basic layout and furnishings as his and Kent's, but she had added personal touches: ferns, ceramic cats, what have you.

Gloria returned from the kitchenette and handed a glass of iced tea each to Earl and Jenny. "Here we go."

Earl took a sip. It was a little weak for his taste. Just the same, he smiled and smacked his lips. With both women staring at him, he focused on his glass. "So, did you brew this yourself, or. . . ?"

"It's instant." Gloria was on the couch, sitting forward anxiously.

"So you just dip the bag. . . ?"

"Crystals. You put crystals in a glass and add water."

"So?" Jenny had waited long enough. "What happened?"

"Nelson is guilty of a lot of things—or he would have thrown me out a lot sooner."

"Why do you say that?"

"He needed to figure out whether I knew enough to be dangerous. Did you get the shredded papers?"

Jenny opened her purse and thin slivers of paper shot out like they were spring-loaded. "All that would fit."

"Good. We need to see whether we can get any of them to fit together. Based on Nelson's reaction to my bluff, some of those may turn out to be the same receipts we found in the record albums."

"Receipts?"

Earl folded his hands. "But there are still some things that don't fit. I'm not sure what I think."

"Why don't you tell us all about it, darlin', and we'll work through it together," Gloria said. "Maybe we can come up with something."

Earl shared the details of his private meeting with Nelson. He gave them the context of the situation, what built up his theories, what his expectations had been going in to see the man. After he had unloaded the whole story, he just sat back in his wheelchair and locked his fingers together.

"We should call the sheriff," Jenny said.

Earl looked forlornly at his empty glass. He looked at Gloria. "I don't suppose you could. . . ?"

"Of course, Blue Eyes. Don't say anything interesting until I get back."

"Hey," Earl said, trying to sound bright and cheerful, "how about we go to the cafeteria and get something to eat?"

She looked at him uncertainly. "Now?"

"Yeah, it must be almost dinnertime. Besides, something about all this excitement has made me hungry."

"Well," Gloria said, "I can make something here if you want."

"I don't want you to go to any trouble."

"It's no trouble, if you don't mind sandwiches. I've got some turkey bologna. Some chicken salad. I can also grill some cheese if you want to wait. And I have some canned tuna fish, if you want."

"Tuna fish?" Earl wrinkled his nose. "The bologna sounds fine to me. If you can put a little mustard on it."

"Sure thing. And you, young lady?"

Jenny smiled. "I'd like mayonnaise, thank you."

"Okay. I'll be right back."

After Gloria left to make the sandwiches, Earl noticed the hum of a clock. He looked over to see a novelty clock on the coffee table, a little replica of the famed Ryman Auditorium in Nashville, home of the Grand Ole Opry.

Jenny clapped her hands together. "I'm just relieved it's all over."

Earl looked at her. "What's all over?"

"Mr. Nelson killed George Kent. All we have to do now is call the sheriff and report him."

Gloria came back out, wiping her hands on a towel. "Do y'all like pickles on your sandwiches?"

Earl thought for second then nodded. "Sure."

Jenny asked, "What kind of pickles?"

Gloria started to answer then stopped herself. She made a crooked face. "Let me check." She disappeared back into the kitchenette.

Earl turned to Jenny. "What do you mean, we just call the sheriff? Why would you think that Nelson killed anyone?"

"But you were the one who said George Kent was murdered. And then Nelson secretly went into Mr. Kent's apartment, so I figured. . ."

"That's been our problem. We've been doing too much figuring and not enough finding."

"But you did find something." She clutched a handful of the confettied paperwork. "If this is what you think it is, it could prove they were running their illegal deal out of Candlewick. Since it's a state-licensed facility, that might make it a felony or something."

Gloria reappeared. "I have sweet pickles, and I have dill pickles."

Earl said, "Dill is fine, I guess."

Jenny's face fell. "No bread and butter pickles?"

"Aren't those the same as sweet pickles?"

"No. They're different."

"Oh. Well then, no. I don't have any bread and butter pickles."

Jenny frowned. "Okay. . .um. . ." She tilted her head. "I guess I'll pass. Thanks."

Gloria smiled then nodded a little uncertainly and disappeared again into the kitchenette.

Earl turned to Jenny. "We have no proof whatsoever that Nelson is the killer."

"Nelson couldn't act more suspiciously if he wore a sandwich board on which he had written out a full confession. What more could you need?"

"For one, we need some kind of evidence. It's going to be hard to pin him as the murderer." Earl frowned. "And that bit about the antifreeze was news to me—if he had killed the man, why tell me something like that?"

Jenny opened her mouth to reply, but nothing came out.

"See?"

"Well, the man is still breaking the law. Murderer or not, he's still a criminal. Right?"

"Here we are!" Gloria came out with two plates, which she set on the small, round dining room table. "Okay, Jenny, yours is there—turkey bologna, mayonnaise, no pickle—and Earl's is there—turkey bologna, mustard, and dill pickle." She set the plates down as she spoke. Then she turned and left for the kitchen.

Jenny said in a low, forceful voice, "You need to call the sheriff's department and report Ed Nelson. They can figure it out. It's what they do."

"Why don't you call them? I don't want to get involved."

"It's a little late for that." She took her chair. "You're involved whether you like it or not." Jenny took a bite of her sandwich. She frowned then checked under the bread. With an awkward smile, she took a knife, cut off the section with her teeth marks on it, and kept that part as she traded plates with Earl.

"But there will be questions. And forms. And paperwork. I hate that stuff."

"We need to get scum like him off the street before he preys on someone else. Think of the victims."

"Isn't gambling a victimless crime?"

"Look at somebody like that poor man Dandy. Doesn't he seem like a victim to you?"

Earl nodded. "I suppose he does."

"Do the residents of Candlewick strike you as having a lot of disposable income they can just throw in a hole and forget about?"

"No." Earl looked at the sandwich on his plate. "How many people do you think have access to that office there?"

Jenny seemed happier with the second sandwich. "Hmf?"

"You know, the doors, the file cabinets, stuff like that?"

"Ask Gloria. She would know."

At this point, the woman herself returned. "Ask me what? Did I forget something?"

"Nothing," Earl said. "We're fine."

Gloria's eyes widened. "Oh—your iced tea!"

Before she left again, Jenny stopped her. "How easy is it for some passerby to just come in and grab something out of the office?"

Gloria stopped to think about it. "Not too easy, I would think. Mr. Nelson keeps his private office locked. And the outer office is always locked when no one is around. All the cabinets are locked up, too." She snorted and said to Earl, "We don't want someone stealing office supplies!"

Earl didn't laugh. He just smiled awkwardly.

"I'll get you that tea." Gloria disappeared into the kitchenette again.

Jenny said, "It's the right thing to do, Mr. Walker. Nelson killed one person, he threatened you, and he fired Grant Caine."

"Well."

"Okay, on the scale of things, Grant's firing is hardly the same, but still. . ." Jenny took another bite of her sandwich.

Earl kept staring at the door to the kitchenette. When Gloria returned, he quickly turned his attention back to his sandwich. Gloria set the glass down for Earl then set a bowl of tuna fish down for herself.

"Anyway," Jenny said, "now that we have this all resolved, we need to figure out your future."

Gloria looked disappointed. "It's all resolved?"

Earl shook his head. "No. Nelson said he didn't kill Kent."

"Of course he said that," Jenny shot back. "Now stop putting this off. It's important to wrap up all this other business so we can turn our attention to finding you a new place to live."

Gloria looked aghast. "You still haven't found a new home?"

Earl tried to think of a suitable reply for Gloria. All he could come up with was, "Not as of yet." He turned his attention to Jenny. "Nelson said he wouldn't have been that clumsy."

"Everyone says that."

"Has it occurred to you what will happen when the sheriff comes and arrests Nelson?"

"Another dangerous criminal will be locked up."

"Without the manager, Candlewick will shut down immediately. Do you really want to put all those poor elderly people out on the street?"

Jenny frowned. "They would put someone else in charge,

wouldn't they? Find a replacement?"

"For ten days? Who in their right mind would take the job of being the brand-new manager of a facility that was going to close down in ten days?"

"No leads at all? You don't have any friends or family to help you find a new place?" Earl shook his head sheepishly. "Not yet."

"Well, when did you plan to figure that out?" Gloria seemed upset. "This isn't something you just figure out on the day this place closes. You need to have—"

"A plan, yes, I get that." Earl was sorry he was short with her, but he was too embarrassed to apologize. Besides, couldn't the woman see he needed to think? He turned back to Jenny. "As the manager, Nelson had so many other avenues open to him. If he was going to murder somebody, he could do it very easily."

"We need to be looking at brochures, making calls, checking the papers," Gloria said. "You need to see what your options are. How can you keep in touch with your friends if you don't even. . ." She didn't finish the sentence. Her lip trembling, she turned her attention to her bowl of tuna fish.

"Fine." Earl set the sandwich down. "I'll start the search."

"But first things first," Jenny said. "Call the sheriff's department, and tell them what you know about Ed Nelson. You have enough to get them started. They are professional people—just give them the lead, and they can take it from there." Earl started to protest, and she added, "It's their job. It's what they do."

"Fine. But I can't do it from here. I need to go home first."

Jenny eyed him warily. "Why? What's wrong with—"

"I'm not comfortable calling from here." He looked at Gloria and tried to smile. It hurt. "No offense. I'd just be self-conscious."

Jenny said, "But you are going to make the call, right?"

Earl hesitated. "Yes."

"You're sure?"

He nodded. "Yes."

"Because if you don't call the sheriff, I will."

"Fine. I'll call."

Jenny smiled reassuringly. "And then we'll see if we can figure out what to do for your move."

Gloria smiled. "Absolutely."

Earl nodded. "It sounds like you ladies have the rest of my life mapped out."

Jenny and Gloria shared a grin. Gloria winked. Jenny said, "We're working on it."

Earl took a deep breath and let it out. "All right then, College. I guess you best get me home so I can do my part for God and country."

"Yes sir!" Jenny got behind his wheelchair and gripped the handles and pushed him around the dining table, toward the door. She turned back to Gloria. "Thanks so much for feeding us!"

"I'm sorry it wasn't more."

"No, it was great."

When the two were out the door, Gloria waved. "Hope to see you soon, Blue Eyes."

Earl returned the wave uncomfortably. He grumbled something.

As Jenny pushed him down the hall, she asked, "So what was that all about?"

"What was what about?"

"That whole weird vibe in there. You were acting very strange."

"Do you think Gloria noticed anything?"

"How could she not?"

Earl gripped the wheels on his chair. "Stop. Go that way."

"But your apartment is—"

"If we went to that computer room, would we be able to go on the worldwide Internet?"

"Um, I suppose so. You can find pretty much—"

"Then we need to make a detour."

CHAPTER TWENTY

Jenny pushed Earl's wheelchair past the chapel entrance. "This isn't just another stalling tactic, is it?"

"Who, me?" Earl tried his most innocent look. Since he couldn't turn his neck far enough, it was a wasted effort. "Like you said, with Candlewick closing, I have to find a new place to live."

"You are going to call the sheriff though, right?" They reached the end of the hall and turned left.

"Sure, sure. Of course I will. Everything in its time."

"I would hate to think you're just putting it off."

They came upon a couple of residents, an elderly man and woman dressed for tennis, carrying their rackets. The two were sharing a laugh. Earl nodded to them as they passed.

Once the two were out of earshot, he turned and said to Jenny, "Besides, how long could I stall?" They came upon a group of people headed the other direction, a man pushing a walker accompanied by a younger woman and three small children. Earl waited until they passed. Once they were gone, he turned his head again. "Fine. I'll make the call. We just have to make this stop first."

They reached the computer room without incident. The light coming through the windows must have created a glare on the monitor screens, because the blinds were almost closed.

Most of the stations were occupied. They headed for the lone open unit, and Jenny moved aside the chair and helped Earl roll his wheelchair into place.

Jenny said, "Do you know what you're doing?"

"Of course I know what I'm doing! I'm not some senile old man who needs to be put out on the trash heap."

"Oh. Sorry. I didn't mean to insult you."

"You're forgiven." Earl rubbed his hands together. "I guess you can tell me one thing."

"What's that?"

"How do I use a computer?"

Jenny tried to offer him a disapproving look. But it soon collapsed into a grin. "All right, Mr. Walker. This is your monitor, this is your mouse, and this is your keyboard. You use the mouse like this to move your cursor—that's the little arrow on your screen there, right?"

Earl grunted. "How do you look something up? This computer is connected to everything, right?"

A voice came from their left. "You can sign up for computer classes, you know." The man at the next computer was an older gentleman in a snazzy golf shirt and shorts. He adjusted his black-framed glasses. "If you're interested."

"I don't get out much," Earl said. "I don't really have a way to get to school."

The woman on their right butted in. "Oh, they have all the classes right here at Candlewick—all about e-mail, about desktop publishing, about—"

"You're forgetting one vital, key piece of information," Earl grumbled. "In a matter of days, this place will be closed down."

The three stared back at him. Without another word, the man and the woman went back to their respective computers.

Jenny leaned in. "You don't have to be so rude about it."

"Who's being rude? I was just stating the facts."

"Well, there's a better way to do it." She wrinkled her nose. "Now, why are they closing this place again? It seems to have everything!"

"You'll have to take that up with the state." Earl pointed at the screen. "Now, how do I look for things?"

She sighed. "Okay, this program here is called your browser. It's how you go to Web sites and blogs and things."

"No need to get fancy."

"Okay, this is your search engine. You type in what you're looking for, and it finds all the different Web pages that have those same words in them. So, what should we look for. . . . Let's try 'retirement living.' And we need local results, so we'll also add 'Kentucky.' "

Jenny typed the words on the keyboard, and Earl saw the letters pop up in the search box. She hit the RETURN button, and a list of pages came up. "And here are the top results for your search." She pointed at the screen. "You have thousands of results here."

"That sounds like so many. How do you know which ones to choose?"

"They're ranked by popularity. So these top ones here are those sites that most people have visited. Do you want to go ahead and click through these top ones?"

"Let me try." He rolled himself closer to the desk and reached for the keyboard.

"You want to make the search even more specific?"

"Something like that." Using the hunt-and-peck method, Earl had to figure out the letters one at a time. He tried one combination of letters and then cautiously hit RETURN. The search engine came back with zero results. He squinted. "What does that say at the top there?"

Jenny looked close at the screen. "It's asking if you mean 'ethylene glycol.' What is that, your medication?"

"Hardly. So how do I choose that spelling?"

"Just take your mouse and click there."

Earl was a little shaky, but he finally got the little pointy thing to click on the blue line. A new page came up. He read the results then took the mouse and moved the cursor to the top result and clicked through. He allowed himself a grin. He could get the hang of this.

Jenny didn't sound so sure. "What are you looking for?"

Earl was scanning the information on the screen. "Just trying to expand my knowledge."

"But we're supposed to be looking for a new home for you."

"We will." He studied the screen, frowning. "How do I go to a different page?"

She showed him how to click back to the results page and then click through to another page. "What, exactly, are you looking for?"

Earl squinted at the screen. "I'm not sure. How do I see this part at the bottom of the screen?"

"This is how you scroll." She took the mouse and clicked the bar on the right of the screen.

"Stop right there." He read for a few seconds then pointed at the screen. "How can I get a copy of this?"

Jenny instructed Earl to move his cursor up to his toolbar,

choose PRINT, sort through his options, and send it to the printer. "It comes out over there."

Earl pulled away from his computer station to wheel himself over to the printer. He craned his head, trying to see under the printer. "How does this thing work?"

Jenny, puzzled, looked from the printer to the computer and back again. "I don't know."

A young woman in a smock and wearing a name tag approached them. "Can I help you folks?"

Jenny smiled. "We're just waiting for a printout, thanks."

Earl pointed and demanded, "How does this work?"

The lady looked at him uncertainly. "Is it not working again? I thought they had it fixed."

"I'm asking how it works. What does it do?"

"Oh. Um, well, you send your information from your computer. You choose to print and—"

"Yes, yes, but once it gets sent here?"

"Well, the information gets sent here. It's all digital. And the printer reads it and prints it out. I'm not sure what you're asking."

"It's like a copy machine, right? It uses fluid?"

"Oh. Um, sure, you can make copies with it, too. And it comes out—"

Earl reached and tried to open the lid. "How do you open this?"

"Sir, I don't think that's a good idea. When you open it while it's in use, papers get jammed, and then you have to call for someone to fix it."

"Where do you keep your copy machine fluid?" Earl looked around, saw a closet door. "Do you keep it in there?" He began wheeling himself toward the door.

"That door is locked at all times."

"So, you have the fluid in there?"

"No. That's where we keep supplies."

"But not the copy machine fluid?"

"Um. No. Why are you asking about this?"

Jenny tried to apologize for him. "He's new to computers and all this, so he's very excited."

"So only the repairman has the fluid?"

"Well, no, we can refill it. We keep the toner and the fluid up at the front office."

Earl whirled his chair around. He grimaced. "But you keep it lying around sometimes, right? Maybe stacked in the corner or out in the hall?"

"No. Never. We don't want anyone to trip over it."

"Or steal it?"

The lady smiled nervously. "I didn't say that."

"But you have had a problem with someone stealing copy machine fluid."

The woman's face became sterner. "I have never heard of such a thing happening."

"I see." Earl's shoulders sagged. He turned to Jenny. "Come on, let's go."

"Here's your printout." She pulled the sheet off the tray and handed it to Earl.

"Thank you." He looked at it like it was bad news then folded it and stuck it in his shirt pocket. "Let's get out of here."

Out in the hall, Jenny asked, "What was all that about?"

"Nothing," Earl grumbled.

"So, we're heading back to your apartment to call the sheriff?"

"We have to stop by the office first."

"Oh. You're going to talk to Nelson again? Try to make him turn himself in?"

"Not exactly."

Jenny and Earl did not speak again the whole walk to the Candlewick office. They passed various residents in the hall. As they reached the front office, they went through the glass doors and Earl wheeled himself up to the counter. The woman greeted him. "Sorry, sir, we're locking up for the day."

"This will just take a second." Earl cleared his throat. "How does one go about borrowing office supplies?"

The woman's smile wavered. "I don't understand what you mean."

"It's a simple question. How difficult is it for someone to come in here and take some office supplies?"

"You can find all sorts of resources at our small business center." She pointed toward the corridor behind them. "If you turn around and head—"

"We just came from there," Earl cut in. "Actually, I was referring to the supplies found in that cabinet." He pointed. "How does one—"

"That's only accessed by office personnel."

"Is it always locked?"

"Yes. Always." The woman gave him a sour look. "I'm afraid you'll have to use the facilities like everybody else. No exceptions."

"I see." Earl's shoulders sagged. "Thank you."

He turned for the exit. Out in the hall, Jenny asked, "What's the matter, Mr. Walker? What's this all about?"

"Just take me home." The rest of the way back, Earl had nothing to say. They went through the common garden outside.

The skies were overcast. On the way to his apartment, they passed some more residents. Jenny greeted each and every one of them. Earl kept in his own little world.

Even as they reached his apartment and they got inside, Earl was still unwilling to speak his dark thoughts. He was trying desperately to come up with another conclusion.

Jenny turned on the lamp by the couch and sat. Earl was hunched in his wheelchair. Staring, but not at anything in particular. She said, "Well, here we are."

Earl didn't reply. He silently pulled the sheet out of his shirt pocket and unfolded it. He stared at it.

"I guess you should go ahead and make that call now."

He grunted. Then he looked up from his page, dazed. "What?"

"You promised to call the sheriff and report what you know."

"Oh." He nodded almost imperceptibly. The two sat in long silence. Finally Earl inhaled deeply and let it out in a resigned sigh. He reached for the phone and set it on his lap. He stared at it for long, wordless moments.

Then he reached for the end table and picked up a card that listed several emergency numbers. He found the entry for the sheriff and slowly pecked out the phone number. Receiver to his ear, he listened to it ring.

"I know you're nervous, Mr. Walker. But you're going to feel much better when it's all over."

He just nodded. His eyes seemed to be misting up. Finally, there was a voice on the other end. He took a deep breath before responding. "My name is Earl Walker, and I want to report a murder. I killed George Kent."

CHAPTER ⛫ TWENTY-ONE

Jenny threw her arms into the air. "Why did you tell the sheriff that? What do you think you're doing?" Hands on her hips, shaking her head, she paced the living room carpet. "Were you pulling some kind of prank?"

Earl, his hands locked together on his chest, was practically curled up as much as the wheelchair would let him. He shook his head slowly. "No."

Finally, she returned to the couch and flopped down. "I just don't understand. Why would you say that? They take those kinds of calls seriously."

He cleared his throat. "Would you just let me handle it?"

"How can you ask that? I think you've lost your mind!" She stood again, turning this way and that, as if considering whether and in which direction to pace again. She stopped and held out her hands. "Have you taken your medication today?"

Earl was taken aback. "What? Of course I have."

"Because if you need your pills or something—"

"I don't need my pills." He checked the clock on the TV stand. "Well, okay, it's almost time for my next pills."

Jenny went to the kitchen, came back with his medicine bottles, and set them on the dining room table. While she went to get him something to drink, Earl wheeled up to the table and fumbled with the caps. She came back and set a glass on the table.

Earl looked at the juice then at the pills in his hand. "I can't drink that."

"It's grapefruit juice. What's wrong with it?"

"It mixes badly with my medication. You can't take pills and grapefruit juice at the same time."

"Oh. I'm sorry." She took the glass back into the kitchen. There was the sound of a cabinet opening and then water running. She returned with a small glass of water. "Is tap water all right?"

"It's fine." he grunted. He took his pills, took the water, and swallowed the whole lot of them.

Jenny sat across the table from him. "So what happens now?" Her face was so sad.

"Maybe you should go. Before the sheriff gets here. It would be better if I faced him alone."

She didn't answer.

Earl locked his fingers together. From where he was sitting, he couldn't see the clock. So he had no idea how long it was before there was a knock at his door.

He swallowed hard, bracing himself to wheel over to the door, but Jenny got up and beat him to it. The man in the doorway was tall, handsome, and wearing a slightly wrinkled tan suit.

The man identified himself to Jenny as Deputy Landon Fisher, of the Fletcher County Sheriff Department. "What seems to be the problem, ma'am? We got a call from this apartment."

He leaned in and murmured something to her. She glanced back at Earl then replied in a low voice. Earl leaned forward, straining to hear them. "Hey! What are you saying?" He quickly wheeled himself up to the door. "What are you talking about?"

The two seemed to be ignoring him. The deputy said, "Well, we still have to check this out. Just in case, you know."

"Whatever you say," she said in a resigned voice. She held the door open. "Please come in. Have a seat."

"Yes," Earl grumbled. "I'm Earl Walker. I need to turn myself in."

The deputy took a chair and pulled out a notebook and a pen. "All right, Mr. Walker, what seems to be—"

"I'm a murderer."

Jenny pleaded, "Don't listen to him!"

Earl nodded in her direction. "Does she have to be here for this?"

Deputy Fisher looked at Jenny, then at Earl, and then at Jenny again. He scribbled something in his notebook. "I think it would be better if she stayed close by." He looked back at Earl again. "Now, who is it you're supposed to have murdered?" He looked around the apartment. "I don't see any bodies lying around."

"I didn't do it just now, you idiot! Kent died on Saturday."

The deputy stopped scribbling. "George Kent? But that really happened."

"That's what I'm telling you! I poisoned him at that party on Saturday, and he died afterward."

The deputy had a serious look. He borrowed the phone and called in to headquarters, asking for someone specific at the station. He got the information he wanted then hung up.

"What did you poison him with?"

Earl folded his hands. He looked down. "I gave him some ethylene glycol."

Jenny frowned. "No! Ed Nelson killed him!"

"Hmm?" The deputy raised his eyebrow. "You mean the director?"

"Yes," Jenny said. "He's running an illegal gambling operation out of Candlewick. Mr. Kent was his partner. They got into an argument and Nelson killed him! Tell him, Mr. Walker."

The deputy looked back and forth between them uncertainly.

Earl said, "She's right about the first part. About the gambling, I mean."

"Yeah," she said. "We're witnesses!"

"You mean to tell me that you gambled on the premises?"

Jenny was flustered. "Um, no, we didn't actually witness the gambling. . .um, Mr. Walker?"

Earl nodded. "Nelson so much as admitted to me that he and Kent were partners in some kind of betting scheme."

"I see." Deputy Fisher stopped scribbling in his notebook. "And did anyone else besides you two hear this conversation?"

"I didn't actually hear them talk," Jenny mumbled. "But Mr. Walker told me about it."

"I see."

Earl held up a hand. "No, you don't see. There is physical evidence. There were handwritten notes that we found hidden in Kent's apartment. And there was the matter of thousands of dollars kept in a metal box."

"And you have the money?"

"No." Earl grimaced. "Nelson has it."

Jenny went to the table and clutched the slivers of shredded paper. "We do have these!"

"I see." The deputy put a hand on his knee. "And so you claim Nelson murdered—"

"I killed George Kent."

"Now why would you do that?"

Earl hesitated. "My reasons are my own."

"I see."

Earl growled, "Would you stop dismissing me? I am not some senile old man for you to humor!" He started rubbing his hands together. "And it wasn't antifreeze. It was copy machine toner fluid."

The deputy furrowed his brow. "The copy machine. . . ?"

Jenny's mouth opened. She dropped onto the couch.

"It is also a source of ethylene glycol," Earl said slowly. "It causes kidney failure. In an old man like George Kent, I thought it would be the perfect murder weapon. He's an old man who doesn't eat right, who smokes cigars—I knew that no one would think twice if he collapsed at a party like that."

"But if you got away clean, why confess now?"

Earl looked away. "It was gnawing at me. Someone should pay." His voice cracked.

Deputy Fisher was scribbling notes again. "And where is this fluid now?"

"I don't have it here."

"Where did it come from?"

"I sneaked into the Candlewick offices. I got into the cabinet—"

Jenny spoke up. "But it's locked!"

Earl shot her a look. "I picked the lock." He waved a hand. "I used a paper clip. I took the toner out of the cabinet. I sneaked it to the party—"

The investigator asked, "How come the office didn't notice it was missing?"

"Oh, right. I went and removed some toner, but I replaced

the, um, can. And I took my toner to the party, where I gave it to the victim."

"Wait," Jenny said, her voice trembling. "Are you talking about the toner or about the fluid? Copy machine toner is like a powder."

Earl thought a second. "The liquid part. Whatever."

The deputy prodded him. "So you, what, used a syringe or something?"

"No. He drank it."

"Just like that?"

"Well, he was eating chili. I knew he would be thirsty. I knew that he didn't drink alcohol. He drank grape juice."

"So you spiked the grape juice?"

"The colors are similar enough; no one saw the difference."

"So, you risked the lives of everyone who drank out of the punch bowl?"

"No, everyone else was drinking rum."

"Well, except for us," Jenny interjected. "We had milk."

"Fine," Earl grumbled. "Everyone but Kent drank something that was not grape juice. Only Kent had the grape juice. I mixed it into his glass right before he got it. He drank it, and he never knew the difference."

"Why didn't he taste it?"

"He was already eating the spicy chili. His mouth was burning. The grape juice was cold, which deadened the taste of the toner."

"I see." Deputy Fisher scribbled something else in his notebook. Then he started tapping the notebook on his knee. "I've got to admit it, your story—"

Jenny stood. "Wait! Mr. Walker, you couldn't have done any of that—you don't even know the difference between copy machine toner and copy machine fluid." She looked at the deputy. "Besides, he was with me the whole time. He doesn't even know his way around the complex. I have to help him around."

"That's not true," Earl grumbled.

"It was true on Saturday." She looked at the investigator again. "He had no idea where the office was, where the chapel was, where the computer room was—and he certainly didn't know George Kent until that afternoon. I was with him the whole time, Officer. He could not have done any of that."

The deputy looked doubtfully from one to the other. "You were at the party he mentioned?"

"Yes." Jenny nodded. "He didn't even touch George Kent's drink. That would have been—" She stopped. Gasped.

Earl shot her a look. "Shut up."

Deputy Fisher looked at Jenny intently. "That would have been. . .who?"

Jenny had her hands over her mouth. She squeaked. "Mrs. Logan."

"Logan who?" The deputy was scribbling again.

Jenny swallowed and forced herself to answer. "Gloria Logan." She looked at Earl, understanding dawning in her eyes. She asked in a small voice, "You really think that Mrs. Logan did it?"

Earl didn't answer. He set his jaw.

"So this is all you have against this Gloria Logan? She had access to George Kent's glass?"

Jenny gritted her teeth. "She has access to the office. She has a key to the cabinet."

The deputy looked at his notes. "The toner, huh?"

"The fluid." Jenny nodded. "And George Kent was giving her a hard time at the bowling tournament."

Deputy Fisher raised an eyebrow. "You were at the bowling alley?"

"No. They had a video game bowling tournament at the recreation center. They played right before the party."

"Hmm." The investigator closed his notebook. "Does this Gloria Logan live here at Candlewick?"

Earl spoke up. "You don't want to talk to her. She's not involved."

"It sounds like she might know something. Where is she?"

Earl shot eye daggers at Jenny. She shrugged apologetically. "I am so sorry, Mr. Walker. But if Gloria might be responsible, we have to do the right thing." She said to the deputy, "I can take you there."

"Don't do this," Earl pleaded. "You're making a huge mistake."

The deputy waved Earl off. "Don't worry, sir. We can take it from here."

Just the same, Earl followed them the whole way. As they passed the other residents in the hall, he wondered whether they knew that the young man in the slightly wrinkled suit was a policeman.

Gloria's apartment was located near the atrium. Near her front door was an ornate stone fountain, vines climbing the sides. When Gloria answered their knock, Earl couldn't bear to go inside. He waited out in the atrium.

Listening to the gurgling of the fountain, Earl wrung his hands. What could they be saying inside there? Why would Jenny have turned on him like that? Why did the deputy allow them to come like this?

Earl shut his eyes tightly. He wished desperately that he knew how to pray. He had never wanted to believe in God so much in his life. His world was crashing down around his ears. He felt like the loneliest man in the world.

After what seemed like an eternity, the door to Gloria's apartment opened. Earl briefly held out a hope that Jenny and the deputy would come out laughing, glad to find it was all a big mistake.

Earl's heart fell when he saw their faces. Gloria was with them. She looked so rattled. As they passed, Gloria looked at Earl. "Do you believe any of this?"

Earl couldn't look her in the eye.

The other three proceeded down the hall, and Earl had to wheel himself to catch up. He asked, "Where you headed now? Downtown?"

Jenny answered, "We're going to Mark Conroy's." She was so sad.

Earl frowned. "Why would you all go there?"

"We're going to see whether he still has the dishes." Jenny looked furtively left and right then leaned closer to Earl. "You know, the dishes from the party."

As the group continued its march, Earl began to recognize his way. Soon they were at the door he knew so well from the previous Saturday.

When he opened his door, Mark Conroy was surprised to see the group. "What's all this?"

Deputy Fisher showed his badge and identified himself. "Sir, I understand you had a gathering on the premises last Saturday?"

"Y–yes. I remember it was Saturday. I had my dialysis right after."

"I see. And would you still have unwashed dishes from that night?"

Earl cut in. "Of course he wouldn't. And if he already washed them—"

"Actually," Conroy said to the deputy, "I haven't washed everything. You're free to come see."

The four followed Conroy through his living room and back into his kitchenette. "The bowls are washed and most of the glasses," he said. "But a few glasses are still there." He pointed to the sink. "I just wash each one as I need it."

The investigator looked at the collection. There were only a few unwashed glasses—three tumblers, what must have been a milk glass, and one glass with a purplish ring around the inside.

"Let's see," Conroy said, "those had the rum, and that one looks like it had milk in it. And this glass had the grape juice in it." He looked over at Gloria and smiled. "You remember, Gloria, that's what George Kent drank."

Deputy Fisher pulled out a handkerchief and delicately picked up the last one. He sniffed it carefully. "It doesn't smell like grape juice."

Conroy made a face. "What are you talking about? What else could it be?"

"Do you have a plastic bag or something?" The investigator pulled the glass close. "This has to be taken in for testing."

Gloria whispered, "What does it mean?"

Deputy Fisher said, "I'm afraid you'll have to come with me until we clear this up, ma'am."

"Am I being. . .arrested?" She was near tears.

"Let's just say you're a person of interest."

Conroy returned with a plastic bag, into which the investigator deposited the glass. He then took Gloria by the arm and headed out. He thanked Jenny and told her that he would be in touch.

As the two left, Gloria looked back at Earl with hurt eyes. He couldn't take it. He looked away. Gloria sobbed as she was led away.

After they were gone, Earl was heartbroken. Conroy tried to ask what it was all about, but Earl seemed to have had the wind knocked out of him.

"I need to leave." He gripped the top rims of his wheels tightly and then exited.

As he was on his way, Jenny soon caught up with him. "Are you going to be okay?"

He didn't answer her. In fact, he didn't speak the whole way back to his apartment. He was too busy fighting the burning sensation eating away at his chest. He wondered if this was what a heart attack felt like.

He reached his apartment. At the door, he crossed inside.

"I know this is so hard for you," Jenny said. "I am so, so sorry."

Earl gritted his dentures. "Don't talk to me."

CHAPTER TWENTY-TWO

Time passed as Earl sat in the dark, hunched in his wheelchair, wringing his hands. How long had it been? He hadn't slept. The minutes had passed into hours. For all he knew, the hours had passed into days. He didn't know what had been on the news; he didn't know how his shows were doing, didn't even know what day it was.

It would have been simple enough to turn on the TV and find all those things out. But he just didn't have the heart. The whole world was outside his door, but as far as he was concerned, it could stay out there.

Deep in his funk, he barely noticed the knock at the door. It was just a small tapping really, hesitant and uncommanding. Whoever it was could go away.

When he heard it again, he wheeled over to the door. He couldn't reach the peephole, but he could peek out the curtain. College girl was out in the hall. Waiting.

Earl paused. There was a third hesitant knock, so he unlocked the door and opened it a crack. "Yes?"

Jenny stood there. "Hello, Mr. Walker. I just came to check on you. See how you're doing." Earl continued to stare, the door still open only a crack. "May I come in?"

Earl looked at her, his hand still on the doorknob. It would be easy enough to simply shut the door and be done with it. He relented. "Fine." He wheeled himself back into the dark living room.

Jenny turned on the lamp and sat on the chair by the couch. "I know what a hard time this must be for you."

Earl didn't answer. He was hunched again, hands locked, staring off into nowhere.

"I can't believe it myself. I think I'm shaking," she chattered. She forced a laugh. "It's like I don't even know how to talk to you anymore. Isn't that silly?"

Earl didn't answer. He didn't even look at her.

"Maybe I should do some cleaning. Would you like that?" Jenny got up from her chair. She stood a second, looking at him. Then she went into the kitchenette and went through the cabinets.

She came back with a rag and a can of furniture polish. She began dusting off the furniture around the living room. She wiped off the lampstand, the end table by the couch, and the credenza. The room was taking on a lemony smell.

"Hey," she said, "remember how I came and you thought I was a maid?" She moved the television set to the left and dusted. "Well, you didn't actually think I was a maid. I know, you don't have maids at Candlewick." She moved the television to the right, dusted. "But I thought you thought I was a maid." She put the TV back in place and looked at him. "Isn't that funny?"

Earl still ignored her, occupied in his own little world. He was like a statue.

Jenny stood a moment, holding the rag. "Do you really want

to stay inside like this? We could go outside."

He shot her a look then turned away from her.

"We don't have to talk to anybody if you don't want to," she continued. "But we could just get some fresh air. We could even just go out to the garden if you wanted. Would you like that?"

He didn't answer.

"It's just so unhealthy to sulk like this, all by yourself in the dark," she continued. "Your spirits will never improve this way."

He still had no answer.

"Hey, I brought you some materials from other retirement communities." She set her backpack on the coffee table, pulled out her Bible, and then dug through the bag until she found a stack of brochures. She set them on the table. When he didn't respond, she went to the TV. "Say, maybe you want to see what's on right now. Would you like that?"

He didn't answer. He didn't even seem to register the question.

She turned the set on, and the screen flickered to life. She went to the end table and grabbed the remote, flipping through the channels. Judge show, midday news report, reruns. "Here, want to pick something?"

She handed him the remote. He looked at it a second like it was some strange object he had never seen. He pointed it at the TV and hit the OFF button. The TV flickered to black.

Jenny sat in the chair again. "I guess I've been stalling. I came here because I have something I need to tell you. I just don't know how to break it to you."

Earl looked at her. "I see." He looked away. Began rubbing his hands together.

"You're such a sweet man; I just hate the idea of hurting

you—any further, I mean." Jenny hesitated then stood again. "Say, would you like me to get you something to drink?"

Earl had nothing to say. He barely noticed her leaving for the kitchenette again. He heard her open a cabinet and grab some glasses. There was the sound of the fridge opening then some pouring. She came back with two glasses of grapefruit juice.

She began to hand him his glass and stopped. "You didn't just take your pills, did you?"

He shook his head and took the glass from her. He took a sip. It was welcome refreshment, but he wasn't going to tell her.

She took her chair again and sipped from her own glass of juice. She made a face but didn't comment. Instead she said, "So, anyway, I came by to see how you're doing."

Earl said, "You wanted to tell me something."

"Oh. Yes." She sipped again from her glass. "I just didn't know how to—"

"Whatever it is, just spit it out. It can't be any worse than what you did already."

"Ouch—I guess I deserved that." Jenny took a deep breath. "Okay, the sheriff's department got the results on that glass. You were right, it was the toner fluid—the test came out 100 percent positive."

Earl considered this. "Why would they tell you that?"

"What do you mean? Why wouldn't they?"

"Isn't it an ongoing investigation? They still have more suspects to interrogate. They still have more leads they have to follow. Right?"

Jenny looked at him with pity. "I'm afraid not."

"But how. . . ?" His voice trailed off.

"I talked to the lady in the Candlewick main office. They came and took all the chemicals out of the cabinet for testing."

Earl tilted his head. His lips moved, but nothing came out. He was trying to say something, but no words came.

Jenny smiled awkwardly. "One good thing—they are also going through Nelson's files. Based on our tip, the sheriff decided it was worth investigating the betting operation he had with Kent."

"So, Nelson has been arrested?"

"Not yet. But it looks like he won't be able to get away with what he was doing. You see? We stopped him before he could set up at some new place and hurt someone else."

"Huh." Earl began wringing his hands again. "So they might still decide he was the one who killed Kent."

Jenny got quiet. Her face turned red. "Well. . ."

Earl noticed. "What?"

She replied in a small voice. "It sounds like they've narrowed their investigation to just Gloria." She sighed. "She seemed like such a nice lady."

He rubbed his eyes. "Just when you start to trust someone. . ." He gripped the wheels on his chair and started rocking, like he wanted to go somewhere but hadn't decided quite where yet.

Jenny asked, "Have you eaten?"

Earl hesitated. Then he slowly shook his head.

She got up and went into the kitchenette. He could hear her banging around, doors opening and closing; the girl was apparently looking in the cabinets, in the refrigerator, in the pantry. After a few minutes of clattering, she came back. "I found some cans of soup. Would you like some soup?"

He seemed to consider the question deeply. He finally nodded lightly, like he could take it or leave it.

Jenny hesitated then went back into the kitchenette. Earl followed her, wheeling himself in after her.

He watched her go back to the cabinets and choose two cans. She used the can opener then poured the contents into two bowls. She picked up the bowls and stood uncertainly, looking this way and that.

Earl frowned. "What are you looking for?"

"Your microwave."

"Don't have one."

"Oh." While she set the bowls down and got out a pan for the stove, Earl wheeled himself back into the living room. He needed something to occupy himself with, but nothing seemed to interest him.

He did not want to go out; he did not want to stay in. He did not want to do anything. He did not want to be anything. He just wished he could go to sleep and wake up and that everything would be different.

But that wasn't going to happen.

"It should be heated in a few minutes." Jenny sat next to him. "You know, you can't turn your back on the human race."

He grunted. "It's done me all right so far."

"You can't blame yourself for what happened." She got up. "I have to check the stove."

Earl stared at the coffee table. He reached for the framed photo of him with Barbara. He wondered what she would have thought about all this.

"Maybe it was self-defense," the girl called out. "We don't have all the facts yet. But I guess that's for Gloria and the courts to work out." The girl returned with a steaming bowl, setting it on the coffee table. "Here. Do you have any TV trays or anything?"

"In the closet." He wheeled closer and looked at the steaming bowl. "You gotta be kidding me."

She returned with a metal tray. "What?"

He looked up at her, squinting. "Chili?"

"What?" Her eyes grew wide. Trembling, she came and looked in his bowl. "I didn't think. . . ."

"I should think you didn't."

"Wait, this isn't chili." She was relieved. "It's stew."

"Huh." It was as close to an apology as he was willing to offer.

"If you want, I can give you the cream of mushroom. That's what I have on the stove now."

"No. This is okay, I guess."

"I try not to eat any red meat. That's why I was making the other soup for me."

"That's all right."

She set the metal tray across his lap then the bowl of stew on the tray. "There you go. Oh—you need a spoon."

Earl stared at his bowl. Chunks of beef. All those vegetables. He couldn't for the life of him remember why he ever bought such a thing.

"Gloria is like that, too," the girl called from the kitchenette.

"Like what?"

Jenny came back with his spoon. "She doesn't eat red meat either. We talked about it at the party."

Earl grunted again. He took a spoonful of his stew and blew on it. While he ate, Jenny got her own soup. She returned and started eating. They were silent several minutes, accompanied only by the sound of metal spoons against china, of the slurping of warm liquids.

"You know," Jenny said between spoonfuls, "in a way, what you did for Gloria is like what Jesus did for you. What He did for all of us."

Earl slurped from his own spoon. "I don't want to hear about it."

"We are all sinners, Mr. Walker." *Slurp.* "We all deserve to die. But Jesus came and paid the price. He died in our place. He died in your place, Mr. Walker."

Earl didn't answer. He just kept slurping the spoonfuls of broth.

"I guess that's what you were trying to do for Gloria, wasn't it? When you figured out that Gloria killed that man, you tried to take her place."

Earl set his spoon on the tray. Stared into his stew. "She is going to get the death penalty, isn't she?"

"We don't know what will happen. Maybe there are extenuating—"

"Stop! Just stop!" Earl found it hard to breathe. He clutched his chest. The girl stood quickly, knocking her bowl over. Soup splattered across the carpet. Earl held up his hand to keep her back. "Just. . .stop."

"Are you all right?"

"I've had enough."

She went for his bowl. "I'll just take that away."

"No, I mean enough of your jabber! I was happy before you came along."

"How could you. . ." Jenny stood there, dumbfounded.

"Maybe you should just leave."

She set his bowl back down and went to the kitchen. She came back with a damp towel and got on her hands and knees to work on the rug.

"Leave it." Earl waved a trembling hand. "Just go away."

Jenny stood back up and gestured with the wet towel. "When I first came here, you were miserable." Her voice was trembling. "You were just a shriveled old man in a wheelchair, sitting all day in front of your television. You were alone, and you hated it."

"Don't give me that. I was happy without God. Without you. Without Gloria."

"That's it, isn't it? If you hadn't met Gloria, she wouldn't have broken your heart. Well, people do bad things, Mr. Walker. People hurt people. We live in a fallen world, so that will always be the case. But like I said, you can't just turn your back on the human race. We must forgive others, because God—"

"Get out!" Earl pointed at the door.

Jenny's face fell, her eyes welling up with tears. "I am so sorry."

"I don't want to hear it." He wheeled for the front door. Fumbling with the knob, his whole body trembled with rage. Finally he got the door open. "Go."

Shoulders slumped, Jenny marched slowly to the door. Crossing the threshold, she turned back. "If you should need something, don't hesitate to—"

"I never want to see you again." He slammed the door. Wheeling himself back into the living room, he saw the scrap of paper on the end table with her phone number. He grabbed the paper and ripped it to pieces.

CHAPTER TWENTY-THREE

Earl was glad to be alone. At least that's what he told himself. He pretended to treasure his alone time. When he was in the halls just to get out of the apartment, he avoided as much contact as he could. The residents who passed him were busy with their moving. They had places to go, things to do. Earl was glad to be rid of them.

As far as he was concerned, the fewer people still at Candlewick, the fewer chances of further complications.

When Earl rolled by the library, the place was almost empty. A sign on the door said all the books were for sale. Earl thought about looking through what was left of the collection but decided he didn't need to start picking up any more junk. When your home is being closed down, the last thing you should do is accumulate more junk.

Anytime Earl decided it was time to go outside for some air, he was glad to do it himself. It was his choice, what he wanted to do. He didn't need someone lecturing him about vitamin D or fresh air or any of that.

He wheeled himself through the common garden. He wandered, so to speak. Eventually he found himself at the parking lot. Residents and their helpers, families, and friends were loading up cars, trucks, and trailers with clothing, knickknacks, and everything. Something about the whole process was depressing.

At his apartment, Earl tried to get back to his normal life. In the mornings he washed his face. Brushed his teeth. Picked out his clothes. All the usual routines.

He was glad to do it all alone. Himself. He didn't need anyone to help him.

He got his own bowl of cereal. Got his own juice. Sat at the table and ate his breakfast. Alone. In peace.

After a few spoonfuls, Earl wheeled for the coffee table. He grabbed one of the photos of Barbara and brought it back to the breakfast table. He ate the rest of his breakfast looking into her eyes.

Afterward he settled in front of the TV. He flipped around the channels awhile—courtroom show, infomercial, cooking show, *click, click, click*. His heart just wasn't in it. Where was a good wrestling match when you needed it?

After a while, he just left it on. It didn't matter what it was. Just moving pictures and sound, something to break the silence.

He started looking for something to read. On the coffee table were the materials College had left when he threw her out. Sitting next to the pile was her Bible.

When he kicked her out, he should have thrown it all out with her. He certainly wasn't in the mood to read any of them now.

Earl looked around for something else, anything else, to read. He flipped through the television listings. When he was done with that, he went for the Candlewick Retirement Community newsletter. He couldn't get a newspaper—they had stopped stocking the machine.

He went through his books. No matter what he tried to read, he just couldn't focus. The television made too much noise, but the chatter comforted him.

After a while, he just needed to get out. First he wheeled himself toward the cafeteria. The whole trip he avoided eye contact with any passing residents. Of course, more and more of them were leaving Candlewick forever. They had their lives to live. And Earl would likely, hopefully never see them again. No point getting friendly now.

The cafeteria was emptier than he expected. Of course, fewer people were using it now. There was barely a line.

Earl got up to the counter. He was looking inside the glass case when he heard a disapproving voice. "Feeling better today, sir?"

He looked up. It was the cafeteria worker from before, when Gloria had made something of a scene. "Oh. Um. Hello. I guess. How are you?"

The woman chewed her gum loudly. "Tell me, what happened to your friend?"

Earl frowned. "I don't know who you're talking about."

"You know—Gloria. How's she doing? Is she okay?"

"She's. . .she's in jail."

"No she's not. She wasn't a flight risk."

"Oh. Then I wouldn't know." He pointed at the casserole under the heat lamp. "I just need some of that."

"Oh. Okay then." She slid the plate toward him.

He set it on his tray. He mumbled his thanks and headed for the checkout. He found a table and sat by himself. He realized he had forgotten any silverware and wheeled over to get some.

When he returned to his table, he was frustrated to discover that some others had taken the next table. But he couldn't think of any casual way to move to a different table, so he kept his focus on the plate of casserole. If he refused to make eye contact, maybe he could make it through lunch.

Then they started talking. "So, why did she do it, I wonder?" The speaker was a grizzled old man in some kind of jumpsuit. "There's always a reason."

"You're telling me." The second man's dark, weathered face sharply contrasted with his loud, flowery shirt. "I heard it was some kind of love triangle that went bad. She was working in the office, you know."

"Was she now?"

"Yeah. She was selling drugs out of there."

Earl slammed his silverware on the table. The men at the next table didn't seem to notice.

"Medication?"

"No—you know, drugs."

"Medication is drugs."

"That's not the kind of drugs I mean."

Earl barked, "You should get your facts straight before you shoot off your mouth."

The grizzled man guffawed. "Just passing along what I heard."

"Then maybe you should improve on your listening skills." Earl pushed back his unfinished plate and wheeled away from the table. The men grumbled behind him.

Flustered, Earl sideswiped the waste can. The men laughed. Earl refused to acknowledge them. He simply wheeled back from the can, repositioned himself, and made his way to the hall.

His next stop was the general store. It barely registered to him that he was getting around Candlewick more comfortably now. Not that he felt comfortable. Not about any of it.

To keep from thinking about his life, to keep from feeling sorry for himself, Earl tried to focus on his stomach. Thanks to those busybodies back at the cafeteria, he had not been able to finish lunch. The plan was to go into the general store, find some canned items, and head back to the apartment.

At the store, a sign posted said the place would be open for business right up to the closing of Candlewick Retirement Community. Inside, Earl avoided the two men talking at the front counter. All the same, they stopped talking and looked at him. The man behind the counter called out, "Not much left, I'm afraid."

Grabbing a basket, Earl pulled his lips into a thin line. "Just need some food." He reached the shelves of canned goods. The selection was limited. While Earl perused the few items available, the voices from the front floated toward him.

"If she was going to kill him, you'd think there'd be a better way to do it."

"I don't know, seems pretty clever to me. Her only mistake was leaving behind the evidence like that."

"Tell me about it! If it were me, I'd have gotten rid of the glass or broken it or something."

"At the very least, run it through the dishwasher."

Earl grabbed whatever cans were within arm's reach and wheeled for the checkout. The two men stopped their discussion long enough for Earl to slam the basket on the counter. "I'll just take these."

"Lessee now. . . ." The grocer emptied the basket can by can. "Corned beef hash, spaghetti and meatballs, turkey chili, tamales—"

Earl scowled. "What?"

The man held up the last can. "Didn't mean to get the tamales, huh? No problem, I can just set them aside—"

"No, what did you say about chili?"

The man went back to the previous can and held it out to Earl. "Yeah, this is turkey chili. Did you not mean to get that?"

Earl snatched back the can. "Turkey chili? Who in the world eats this?"

"We don't get a lot of call for it," the man answered. "But some people don't want to eat red meat, so this is a substitute." He turned to the other man. "You know who special ordered this? Gloria Logan."

The other man chuckled. "You don't say."

"A little less of the chatter, please," Earl grumbled. "Just let me check out and go."

Back at his apartment, Earl set his cans on the counter in the kitchenette. He fumbled with the can opener but decided he wasn't hungry anymore and gave up.

He wheeled back into the living room. Earl just didn't know what to do with himself. He reached for the television remote, decided against it. Reached for a book, decided against it. He sat and stared at nothing for long moments. Seconds, minutes, hours? He had no idea.

Eventually his eyes focused on the coffee table. The pictures, the pamphlets, the Bible. Earl reached for the brochures Jenny had left behind, options for new living arrangements. He looked at the pictures of old folks having the time of their lives— laughing, hugging, dining, dancing. He went through the various brochures, comparing and contrasting the various options offered by each place. Swimming. Hiking. Workshops. Events.

Earl looked down at the picture of Barbara. "What do you think, baby?" He held out the pamphlets. "This one apparently is for people who go in for a lot of water sports. This one is great for people who want to make their own pot holders."

Earl chuckled to the empty room. Then he grew silent, rubbing the brochure in his hand. Joke or no joke, time was running out. He really did need to find someplace to live.

He thought about the girl. Jenny Hutton. She only meant well. She went to the trouble of tracking down all these brochures for him. She had gotten the newspaper, had circled the listings for him. She only wanted to help.

Maybe he had been hard on her. But then he thought about the chain of events over the past week or so. How she pestered him into getting out. Into meeting those people. Into meeting Gloria.

"I still can't believe it," Earl said. He looked at Barbara's photo. "There is no way that woman could have done it. No way."

He shook his head. Thought about all his years on the bus. All those years learning to observe. Learning to judge a situation. Learning to judge characters.

"That woman did not kill that man. Gloria Logan did not kill George Kent."

All right, hotshot, Earl told himself, *how do you explain the facts? Everything is stacked against Gloria. She doesn't stand a chance.*

Earl threw the brochures down and started wringing his hands. He felt that tightness in his chest again. He shut his eyes tight, trying to squeeze out the world.

When Earl finally came back out of the darkness, his eyes locked onto the Bible on the table. He stared at it.

Finally he reached out and picked it up. The leather cover was smooth. He ran his finger along the gold lettering. With bony, withered fingers he opened the book and let it flop open on his lap. He began reading in the middle of the page. But he found his thoughts were still racing like a runaway train.

> "Vindicate me, O God, and plead my cause
> against an ungodly nation;
> rescue me from deceitful and wicked men."

Poor Gloria, probably headed for a jail cell. Will she have to stay there until her trial?

> "You are God my stronghold. Why have you
>   rejected me?
> Why must I go about mourning, oppressed by
>   the enemy?"

Will she get many visitors there? Will her family visit her there?

> "Send forth your light and your truth,
> let them guide me; let them bring me to your
> holy mountain, to the place where you dwell."

What if I tried to visit her? Would she even talk to me, after what I did to her?

> "Then will I go to the altar of God,
> to God, my joy and my delight.
> I will praise you with the harp,
> O God, my God."

How could things have gotten this bad? How can a man who just wants to be alone get so entangled with other people's problems?

"Why are you downcast, O my soul?
Why so disturbed within me?
Put your hope in God, for I will yet praise him,
my Savior and my God."

Earl broke down and cried. He closed his eyes and bowed his head. He wasn't quite sure how to begin, so he just dove right in. "God, I don't really know You. But I know some people who speak very highly of You."

He opened his eyes and looked around. The room remained silent. Well, what was he expecting?

Earl bowed his head again, closed his eyes. He cleared his throat. "I'm in such a bad way. I've done a horrible thing to such a wonderful woman. I don't know who committed this murder— but it could not possibly have been Gloria. She couldn't have."

Earl listened again. Nothing. Was he doing this right?

"I have been alone for so long. . .I don't even know what it's like to reach out to anyone. But I'm reaching out to You now. Please meet me where I am."

Head bowed, eyes closed, Earl just sat in the quiet living room. He wasn't sure how prayer was supposed to work. Did he say the right words? Was there some chant or some secret code word he should have spoken?

Where was his mind supposed to go? What was he supposed to focus on?

Eyes closed, he tried his best to meditate. But the events of the past few days kept creeping into his thoughts.

Was this the voice of God? Was this how He spoke to people?

In his mind, Earl saw flickers of memory. That day on the bus when he was shot. The day Barbara died. The day Earl decided he no longer wanted to walk. The day that he got dropped off at Candlewick, abandoned by his last friend in the world. How Jenny Hutton started coming to visit him. The bowling tournament in the recreation center.

Earl's thoughts turned to Gloria. Her red hair. Her sparkling eyes. Her girlish laugh. Her sweet disposition.

The flickers of memory darkened as he was reminded of all the evidence against her. Motive. Means. Opportunity. Even the glass tested positive for copy machine toner. She was caught dead to rights.

One hundred percent.

Earl opened his eyes. Wait a minute—that couldn't be right. If that glass was the murder weapon, the test would have come back some percentage toner, some percentage grape juice.

Gloria Logan was not the killer.

Earl started wringing his hands again. She was a prime suspect in a murder—and it was his fault. He needed to clear her name.

He gripped the wheels on his chair, ignoring his sore hands. He had no destination, so he started spinning slowly in a circle while he tried to choose what to do next. He could head for the telephone. He could head for the door. He could head for the kitchenette.

He was getting nowhere fast.

Finally Earl decided he needed to get out. He needed to find some things out—and quickly. The clock was ticking for Candlewick Retirement Community, and all the likely candidates for murderer were packing up and moving to the four corners of the earth. Any minute now the murderer would be gone, if he or she wasn't gone already.

Earl got outside the apartment. He was so flustered he got one of his wheels caught in the doorway. Some passing children laughed. The old man with them shushed the kids and gave Earl an embarrassed smile.

But he couldn't worry about that now. First things first. Earl had to reconstruct his and Jenny's wandering, accidental tour from that Saturday. It took some doing for him to remember every false start, every wrong turn.

Eventually he hit them all: the library, the chapel, the general store, the computer room. He ended up at the recreation center. It saddened him to see how empty the room had become. What had so recently been a thriving place of bustling activity was now a quiet, nearly empty room with just a few people busy at very few activities. The video machine was unmanned, the accompanying TV screen dark. The billiard table was unoccupied. At one table, a man was assembling a jigsaw puzzle. At the card table, a group of four played dominoes.

Earl looked around the room carefully. He closed his eyes and went back to that room on that fateful Saturday. He mentally reconstructed it all. Meeting the bowlers—Dandy Anderson, Ray Stanton, Mark Conroy, Sally Brouwer. . .and Gloria Logan.

He turned his memory to the other parts of the room. He tried to remember all the games, all the activities, all the faces. He remembered the moment Kent came to his attention. In his memory, Earl focused on the other faces as people reacted to Kent—with anger and with terror and with resignation. How Kent ruined the game at the billiards table, how everyone held their breath as he crossed the room, how he came and interrupted the bowling tournament.

Earl fought to remember everything that was done. Everything said. He remembered Kent taking off his ring.

Once he got it all reenacted in his mind, he turned his attention to when the group got up to go. They were going to the party.

Earl followed the hall back to the site of the party. Along the way he forced his memory to reconstruct that trip. The people they met. Who stopped to talk with their host. How they passed Kent talking with Ed Nelson.

Earl reached Conroy's apartment. He considered knocking and asking to come in but didn't know how he would explain himself. Besides, the man was busy finishing his packing for the move. So Earl contented himself with parking across the hall and imagining the party. Hunched in his chair, eyes closed, head tilted upward, one hand waving in the air like a conductor's, Earl mentally pictured the entire affair.

Kent arriving. Where he sat. Where he put his ring. What he smoked. What he ate. What he drank.

Earl returned home no closer to figuring things out. Depressed, he sat in the living room. He saw the afghan still balled up on the couch and decided that he had waited far too long to wash it. In fact, with all the excitement these past several days, he hadn't done any laundry at all.

He wheeled himself to the couch and pulled out the afghan. As it slid across the coffee table, there was a noise, and an object dropped to the carpet. Earl squinted and saw it was Kent's ring.

"Huh." He let go of the afghan and reached for the ring. From up in his chair, it took some doing, but he finally got it.

He took it over by the end table and switched on the lamp.

Looking at it up close, holding it in the light, it wasn't nearly as impressive as he had expected. The metal was dull pewter, and while the white stone was enormous, it was merely a peridot. For all the interest everyone had shown, Earl would have expected it to be a diamond or something.

He turned the ring this way and that, watching the light bounce off the birthstone from different angles. Then a thought hit him, and he jerked suddenly, nearly dropping the ring.

As the thought made its way through the circuit, Earl grinned. Of course. It seemed fantastic, almost bizarre—but it was the only possible explanation.

But he had a problem. He couldn't just call the sheriff's office—he had already made a fool of himself. They would never believe him now.

He couldn't take it to Candlewick management. Whether or not Nelson had officially been arrested, he'd hardly be in the mood to listen to anything Earl had to say.

How about the press? As nifty as that sounded, Earl had no idea how to even pursue such a thing. What was the procedure? What number did you call? Who would you ask for? No doubt it would be a simple thing if Earl had a moment to research the idea. But he was in something of a hurry.

No, there really was only one person he could call. Earl scrambled to find the number. After several minutes of fruitless searching, it finally came to him where it was.

Thanking God he had not put out his trash for, well, several days, Earl went to the kitchenette, grabbed the receptacle, and dumped it out on the dining room table. He pawed through the refuse until he found one, two, three, then four scraps of white paper.

He pushed the torn pieces around on the tabletop, attempting to reconstruct their original formation. An important piece still missing, he pawed through more trash, his hands getting sticky. He wiped his hands on his pants and tried again.

Finally he found the last jagged scrap of white paper. Returning to his homemade jigsaw puzzle, he placed it in the hole to complete the original picture: Jenny Hutton's phone number.

CHAPTER TWENTY-FOUR

It was late in the afternoon before Jenny could get there. They didn't speak as Jenny wheeled Earl the whole way down the walk. His hands were trembling too much for him to roll himself. At the door to the apartment, she stopped and looked at him tenderly, brushing the hair off his forehead. "Are you sure about this?"

"Go on." Earl grunted. "You know what to do."

She smiled uncertainly. "I can stick around if you want."

He didn't smile back. "I have to do this myself."

She looked at him for a long moment. "Well, you know where I'll be."

Jenny left him. As the echo of her steps drifted into the wind, Earl turned his attention to the convoy of movers. Primarily teens, by his reckoning, they carried, carted, and slid boxes, odds and ends, and small furniture out of the apartment and across the grass toward the parking lot.

One freckled kid in a striped shirt gave Earl a friendly grin. Earl tried to return the smile, but he didn't feel up to it.

Alone in the courtyard, he was aware of how empty the complex had already become. Soon everyone would be scattered to the four winds. Sure, for some it would only mean a few miles in one direction or another. But for those residents of Candlewick who weren't so mobile, it was almost like being transferred to Egypt or Antarctica.

He sat for long minutes, soaking up the world. The sun was warm. The air was cool. The smell of honeysuckle wafted to him.

He would miss that most of all.

Turning his attention to the apartment in question, Earl heard sounds coming out through the open door—the clunking of objects, the scrunching of paper, the taping of boxes, the cursing at things not fitting as conveniently into boxes as hoped.

Earl heard a grunt, and out came a man carrying three stacked boxes. Struggling with the weight, the man had to look around his payload to see where he was going.

Earl rolled back out of the way. Even so, the man nearly stumbled into him. "Oh! Sorry."

"You shouldn't try to carry so much." Earl hoped he didn't come off as gruff as he thought he sounded. He added, trying a softer tone, "You'll hurt your back."

"Uh-huh." The man just kept going, stumbling across the grass toward the parking lot.

Earl, hands still shaky, wheeled delicately toward the door. He heard voices from inside, belonging to a man and a woman. Reaching the threshold, he called out. "Hello!"

A woman whom Earl remembered as Conroy's daughter came to the door, her hair tied back. She gripped a long lamp. "Hello! I guess you're here to see Dad?"

Earl tried his best smile. "Yes, ma'am."

She turned and yelled. "Dad! One of your friends." She smiled at Earl, holding out a hand. "Remember me? I'm Clara. We met at the rec center."

"Earl." He took the hand. "Good to see you again."

"You, too." She went back in, and the door was soon filled with Conroy in gray sweat clothes. He looked at Earl and dropped his grin. "Oh. Come to see me off?"

"Something like that."

"It'll be a relief to get out of this place. I don't know why any of us fought to stay." He chuckled. "If it weren't for my daughter and her family. . ."

"Yeah." Earl glanced around and saw the kids and the man returning from the parking lot. He turned back to Conroy. "I was hoping we could have a few words."

Conroy thought for a second then shrugged. "Why don't you come in? I think I have some juice."

Clara's voice called out, "Dad, where do you want this?"

Conroy went back in. Earl wheeled inside, where father and daughter discussed a novelty plate of some sort. Earl never gave much thought to such knickknacks, so he couldn't follow the conversation. To him a plate was a plate.

Finally, Conroy turned his attention back to the man in the wheelchair. "Look, I know it's hard to let go and all, but we've got to get moving."

"I really want to speak to you for a few minutes." Earl glanced at the woman stuffing crumpled newspapers into a box of packed dishes. He looked back at Conroy. "Alone."

Conroy eyed him. Finally he said coolly, "You'll have to visit me at the new place. We can talk then."

"Oh." Earl reached into his shirt pocket and pulled out a slip of folded paper. "I almost forgot."

"What's this?"

Earl shrugged. "A note."

Smiling tentatively, Conroy unfolded the paper. He glanced at Earl before turning to the words in the brief message. Slowly, his eyes narrowed. His brow furrowed.

The message was short. Conroy moved his lips silently as he read it to himself again and again. The blood drained from his face. His shoulders dropped several inches. Turning to the woman in the corner of the room, Conroy tried to speak. A croak came out. He tried again. "I have to step out."

"Daddy? What's wrong?" Clara stopped with the box. "Are you all right?"

"I think it's just the move." Conroy pulled a handkerchief from his pocket and dabbed his forehead. He forced his shoulders back up. "The exertion is getting to me."

"Maybe you should sit down."

He scooted around behind Earl's wheelchair and gripped the handles. "Actually, we're going out for some air."

"Good. We'll wrap things up in here. You go sit somewhere and relax."

Conroy pushed Earl outside, across the courtyard, and down to the main hall. When they entered the recreation center, he shoved the chair hard across the room. Earl had to grab the wheels to stop from crashing into the card table. By the time he got turned around, Conroy was pacing the big room, making circuits across the red patterned carpet.

The empty room was silent. No card games. No billiards. No TV.

Earl stared at Conroy. He didn't say anything.

Conroy, pacing, working his fingers together, stopped in front of the big glass doors leading back outside. Looking out over the lawn, he finally croaked, "How did you know?"

Earl opened his mouth but found it too dry. Until that moment he thought he had it all worked out. But he now realized he still didn't quite know the words to say.

So he started rambling, just to see where it led him. "You know, when we get to a certain age, we begin to think we understand death. We may not like it. We may not welcome it. But we think we understand it. After we watch our friends and loved ones pass on, we think we expect it."

Conroy, forehead pressed against the window, didn't say anything.

Earl continued. "We learn things about people. Like about Kent. None of us liked him, and it turned out some of us hated him. Heck, it turned out a lot of people hated him."

Conroy turned. Nodded. "Sure."

"We get so used to our routine. Every day we do things in a certain way, at a certain time. It's been that way—exactly that way—for so long that you forget life isn't really like that. This facility had a mission to protect us from life. To insulate us from it." Earl stopped, locking his fingers together. "But life has a way of breaking through."

Conroy stared down at the carpet.

Earl added, making sure he still had his audience, "You know?"

Conroy walked over to the pool table, his eyes glassy. "Sure." He began putting the hard colored spheres on the felt table.

"Suddenly, this place we have all come to trust is going away. And, even more suddenly, one of our own is taken from us. Not by life or the elements or God or anything natural or normal or acceptable." Earl cleared his throat. "The routine is broken."

Conroy went over to a wall by the billiards table and picked out a cue from the rack hanging there.

Earl glanced around at the big empty room. Calculated how far he was from the exit. He began slowly rolling his chair, a little at a time, toward the glass door that led outside. Just in case.

He continued. "At first, the sheriff and everyone else just saw another old man die. Nobody thought anything about it. After all, in a place like this, it happens all the time."

"You thought something about it."

Earl chuckled grimly. "Sure I did. But I didn't want to get involved."

"You got involved."

"It's a long story."

Conroy started to make a shot then must have decided he didn't want to play pool after all. Throwing the cue down, he giggled. "We seem to have the time."

"The problem is that as we began to peel back the layers of George Kent, we discovered just how despicable a man he was. As each new thread presented itself, we tried to follow it to the logical conclusion. We tried to follow the money—both figuratively and literally. Everyone assumed that Kent's career as a blackmailer was what got him killed."

"Everyone? It seems to me that only you knew that George was murdered."

"Well. . ."

"But blackmail seems as good a motive as any." Conroy went over to the dartboard, collected the darts.

Earl nervously inched a little closer to the glass door. "But it turned out that it wasn't about blackmail after all—it was about horse racing. Kent had a whole gambling operation running here, and he got his claws into all kinds of folks out here at the old retirement home."

"Somehow I'm not surprised. With the old gang breaking up, maybe somebody panicked. Maybe somebody was worried about what would happen when George got to some new place. Whether he'd call in any outstanding debts."

"I'm sure that's exactly what someone thought. But you were the one who was poisoning him."

Conroy sputtered indignantly. "Wh–what do you mean? How could I do that? I was never even alone with Kent. When would I have the chance?"

"I'm not saying it wasn't a brilliant plan. You made sure you were always with other people. You arranged for a weekly dinner party. You arranged for Ray to make his fancy homemade chili in your kitchen."

"Y–you're saying I poisoned him that night? I wasn't anywhere near him. Someone else gave him the chili."

"But the poison wasn't just in *his* bowl—it was in the whole batch."

"We all ate it. Are you saying I poisoned myself?"

"That is exactly what I am saying. You poisoned everybody." Earl locked his fingers together. "That was the brilliant part. The murder weapon was not the poison."

"That's crazy. Everybody else was—"

"Stop it, Conroy. I know what you did. And I know how you did it."

"Fine. Tell me, if you're so smart. What do you think I did?"

"You had a group over for dinner every week. Ray made his special chili. Gloria had special dietary needs, so you fixed a separate dish. It was Ray Stanton's recipe, but it was your pot, on your stove—you added the ethylene glycol. Everybody at the party ate the poisoned chili together—that way, when George eventually got sick, you had an alibi. You were nowhere near the man."

"But if—"

"The important part is that you always followed the chili with your secret stash of liquor. But George always had his grape juice. Of course, the significance is not what was *in* the grape juice—it's what was *not* in it."

Conroy trembled. His lips moved, but he didn't say anything.

"According to the Internet, the thing about ethylene glycol is that its effects are evaporated by alcohol. Anyone who had the chili and drank alcohol was fine—one canceled out the other. But for anyone who had the chili and drank something nonalcoholic—for example, grape juice—the poison stayed in his system. In small amounts each time, of course, but it accumulated in him. You were taking a risk already, and you yourself certainly didn't want to have to eat a lot each time. After all, the liquor—the antidote—could have killed you as easy as cure you."

"You certainly have an imagination."

"Gloria didn't drink, but that wasn't a problem—since she didn't eat red meat, she never even tasted your chili. Hers was prepared separately."

Conroy puffed himself up. "Let's say you're right; somebody was sneaking something into the chili. Maybe Ray put it in. Or Gloria."

"You were the ringmaster in control of the situation. You made sure your guests always had alcohol after their chili, and you made sure that George Kent did not."

"Fine, but if it was poisoned, why didn't somebody taste it?"

"Because of Ray's deadening taste buds, his recipe was extremely spicy. It covered the taste of anything foreign in it."

Conroy didn't say anything to that.

"And I should congratulate you on that little party trick here at the rec center." Earl nodded toward the space in the wall where the knife had stuck. "You had Jenny running around looking for some idiot who'd be crazy enough to throw a knife across a crowded room. But the solution was so much simpler—you had the knife all along. You stuck it in the wall yourself."

Conroy held out his hands, while he pouted his lower lip. "I'm no good with that kind of stuff. You saw how badly I did the illusion with the coasters."

"You did it badly on purpose," Earl replied. "That is, unless your grandson really does have quarters growing out of his ear."

Conroy looked at his hands then folded his arms.

Earl continued. "But even after I figured out the means and the opportunity, I couldn't really figure out the motive. Until I found this." Earl reached under the blanket across his lap and pulled out Kent's pewter ring. "Some of the others no doubt thought it was worth a lot of money. But you wanted it for a different reason, didn't you?"

Conroy looked down at the note in his hand again. He read it again.

Does Clara know that Kent is her father?

He looked up, his eyes moist. "How did you know?"

"I didn't. But I knew you must have thought it." Earl leaned in and spoke in a low voice. "When did he tell you that she was his daughter and not yours?"

Conroy paused, choosing his words. Finally he said, "Early in our marriage, Kay and I had. . .difficulties. I was wrapped up in my work. I was never home. So then she came to me and told me she. . ." His voice broke up.

Earl let the silence hang in the empty room.

Conroy wiped his nose with his palm. "Kay had an affair. She told me. She never told me with who. I didn't want to know." He began breathing hard, fighting off sobs. "It was a wake-up call. We went to counseling. We decided to make it work. She said she never saw the man again."

"But. . ."

"But we found out she was pregnant."

"Clara."

Conroy jerked his head then nodded. "We never knew for sure whose child she was. We never spoke of it."

"So how does Kent come back into the picture?"

"I hadn't seen him for years, until he showed up at Candlewick. Whenever Clara and her family came around, he always showed an interest. He was all smiles for her. Then one day, he dropped a bombshell on me."

"He claimed she was his daughter."

Conroy stopped pacing. He just nodded.

"Let me guess—her birthday is in August." When Conroy looked at him, Earl held up the ring again. "This is the August birthstone, peridot. Kent's file says his birthday is in May. So it must have been hers. You and Sally both came around asking about the ring. She wanted it because she's a. . .because she has a problem. But you wanted it because it was the source of so much pain every time Kent showed it to you."

Conroy just nodded, so Earl continued. "And your daughter has the same blood type as Kent—even though you and Kent both needed kidneys, she was a match for him but not for you."

The other man nodded slowly. "At first I refused to believe it. But too many things added up. And then he began squeezing me for money, or else he would tell her."

"A blood type is hardly conclusive evidence," Earl said. "It could be a coincidence."

"I could just tell from his manner it wasn't a bluff. And then last month, when Candlewick announced that it was going to shut down, he said he was going to go ahead and tell her. Maybe he was lying, but I just couldn't risk it."

"Couldn't risk what?"

"Look at us! Look at what's happening to us! All we have, all the people we even know anymore are here in this place. Here at Candlewick."

"And outside, all you have is your daughter and her family."

"They are all I have. They're my only contact with the outside world. If Kent was suddenly her father and I was just some old man. . ."

"Clara would not abandon you," Earl said. "Whether or not Kent turned out to be her biological father, you raised her. You should have trusted her."

"I wasn't thinking straight. I just couldn't bear the thought of being alone."

"So you started your weekly farewell parties. And each week you poisoned Kent just a little more."

Conroy rolled the eight ball across the table. It fell in the corner pocket. "Why come to me? What do you hope to get out of it?"

"I didn't think there should be a big scene in front of your daughter—or your grandchildren. This will be a big enough shock for them as it is." Earl rolled his chair a couple of inches closer toward the door. "I thought we could just talk a little. Once you saw how things were, I was sure you could face it calmly. Then you could tell Clara in your own way."

"Then the sheriff?"

"A deputy is outside. Waiting." Earl nodded toward the door. "In the lobby."

"I'm surprised he didn't storm in."

"All we told him is that you want to make a statement." Earl regarded Conroy. "Don't you?"

"So. . .he doesn't know what you know?" Conroy seized a pool cue, sizing it up.

"You have a chance to turn yourself in." Earl nervously reached for his wheels. "It's the best way."

"I don't know about that." Conroy was considering the weight of the stick in his hands. He flipped it around, so the thick end was up. He took a practice swing. "I wouldn't let Kent ruin my life. I don't know why I should let you."

Earl's hands stiffened on his wheels as he gauged the distance to the exit. How fast could he turn around? Did he even have a chance to get out?

His thoughts were broken by a woman's voice from the hall. "Is everything okay in here?" It was Conroy's daughter, Clara.

Conroy looked up, and all the menace drained from him. "Oh, um, sure, sweetheart." He looked at Earl.

Earl said, "We were just talking. Your father is going out to the lobby now to speak to somebody." He looked at the other man. "You have something to tell him, don't you?"

Conroy set the stick on the table. Taking a deep breath, he stood up to his full height and adjusted his jacket. He exhaled and looked toward the hall. "Yes. I suppose I do."

Earl handed him the ring.

CHAPTER TWENTY-FIVE

Earl had some trouble getting his day started. He was exhausted, he was sore, and he was, oddly, still a nervous wreck. When he poured out his cereal and milk, he barely got them into his bowl. When he brushed his teeth, he dropped them behind the bathroom sink and had the worst time digging them back out. When he got his pills, his hands were shaking so bad he could barely get them out of their bottles.

It should have been easier than this. After the events of the previous day, the murder of George Kent resolved, Earl had expected to sleep better. But he had slept in fits and starts, tossing and turning all night long.

Earl thought himself free to get on with his life. What more could there be to do?

When someone came to his door, he almost jumped out of his wheelchair. When he peeked out the curtain, he was relieved to see Jenny.

When he opened the door, she was all smiles. She had also brought someone with her. "Hello, Mr. Walker," she said, "I brought someone to meet you!"

The man, whom Earl judged to be in his thirties, was dressed in a blue button-down shirt and black pants. He offered Earl his hand. "Hello sir, I'm Andy Benton. I'm the pastor at Jenny's church."

Earl grunted something positive and let them in. He wheeled back into the living room and motioned for them to sit on the couch. "So. . ." He struggled to think of some suitable greeting. Finally he finished the sentence with ". . .how are you?"

Jenny smiled. "I'm doing well, thanks. How are *you*? I know it's been like a roller coaster these past few days."

Earl flexed his hands and smiled. "It's going to take some time before I can get back to normal, I guess."

She chuckled. "I'm just glad all that murder business is past us now. You should be very proud."

"I just made a mess. Sometimes I wish I had stayed out of it. . . ."

"Mark Conroy would have gotten away with murder. You did a great thing." She reached out and brushed his knee. "Now, we have to find you a place to live." Jenny pulled her backpack around to her lap. "I did some research online, and I have some printouts here that might help."

Earl couldn't look her in the eye. "I appreciate all your help. I don't quite know what I'd do without you." He glanced around at all his worldly possessions. "As it is, it will be quite a chore to get all this stuff moved. Even after we figure out where it's all going."

Pastor Benton grinned. "Actually, that's why Jenny brought me out to meet you today, Mr. Walker. She told me about your situation, and I wanted to invite you to come stay with my family until you find a new home."

Earl had a lump in his throat. "W–what?"

Jenny said, "And the college group at church is going to help you pack."

The pastor added, "And we can store all your things at the church until you get settled."

Earl looked from the pastor to Jenny and back again. "Why would you all do so much? You don't even know me."

The pastor winked. "Because Jesus said, 'Whatever you did for one of the least of these brothers of mine, you did it for me.'"

"I don't know what that means."

Jenny grinned. "It means we're supposed to help you. Besides, *I* know you—and I think you're worth helping."

Earl didn't know what to say.

The pastor frowned. "Although, to be frank, I don't understand why the state would shut Candlewick down. There seems to be so much here!"

Earl shrugged. "You'll have to take that up with the state."

Pastor Benton checked his watch. "Well, I have to visit a couple of the other residents. I just wanted a chance to say hello, Mr. Walker. It was fine meeting you!" He held out his hand.

Earl took the man's hand and shook it. He smiled. "It was nice meeting you, too."

"We'll talk again soon!"

After the pastor left them, Earl wheeled himself to the coffee table. "By the way, College, you left your Bible here the other day."

"*That's* where it is! I was looking for it."

"Here you go. I read through it a little."

"You did?" She gave him a curious smile.

"It came in. . .handy." Earl's face grew hot.

Jenny put the Bible in her backpack and set the printouts on the coffee table.

Earl asked, "So, how is your Grant Caine doing? He just seemed to disappear."

"I wouldn't know." Jenny curled a strand of hair behind her ear. "But that deputy was something, wasn't he?"

Earl didn't have any reply to that.

Jenny directed his attention to the printouts. "We can start looking for your new home—as soon as you wrap up one more item of unfinished business."

Earl looked at her. "And what would that be?"

"Have you spoken to Gloria yet?"

Earl rubbed the back of his neck. "I don't think she wants to talk to me. Not after all that happened."

"I know she would love to hear from you."

"I don't know about that." Earl folded his hands together and stuck out his lower lip. "I'm afraid that bridge has already been burned."

"How can you say that?"

Earl held out his hands. "I made a fool out of myself."

"No you didn't. If anything, you tried to do the right thing."

"It doesn't matter what I tried. All that matters is what happened. I'm the one who called the sheriff. I laid out the case. I pointed them right to her."

"It turned out okay in the end."

"Yes—in the end," Earl growled. "But in case you've forgotten the middle part, Gloria Logan could have been convicted of murder. And I would have been the star witness for the prosecution." Earl's voice was now a hoarse whisper. "How can I face her after all that?"

"You need to give Gloria a chance."

"I'm giving her the best chance in the world—I am staying out of her way and giving her a chance to get as far away from me as possible. With Candlewick closing, all I have to do is sit tight and wait until she moves away."

"So, you're going to let her go, just like that? You can't let Gloria leave without some sense of closure."

"She would never forgive me."

"Shouldn't you let her decide that?"

Earl locked his fingers together and looked at the floor. He took in a deep breath and let it out slowly. "I'm going to make some tea. And then we can look at those papers you brought." He wheeled for the kitchenette.

"If you don't do this, you'll always regret it," Jenny called after him. "You can't just avoid her!"

"Watch me!" Earl grabbed onto the counter and pulled himself up. He reached for the cabinet and got out two cups and a pan. He put water in the pan and set it on the stove to boil. While he waited for the water to boil, he got out some peppermint tea.

For years now, Earl had always had tea for an upset stomach. It was a habit he picked up from Barbara. She always loved to sit down with a cup of hot peppermint tea.

What did Gloria think about peppermint tea? What did she think about life, about love?

What did she think about Earl?

He put the question out of his mind. The idea of letting Gloria get away made him feel like he was getting rid of a part of himself.

But after years of being alone—adamantly so—Earl was well practiced in cutting off his nose to spite his face. He just needed to hold on. Sit tight. Strap in and just wait out the storm.

As the water started to boil, Earl tried to ignore the ache in his heart. Just hold on. Sit tight. Wait it out.

Soon Gloria Logan would be gone. Her family would help

her get packed, get her belongings moved, get her relocated. She would have a new home, she could make some new friends.

And Earl's life could go back to normal. He poured the boiling water into the cups. He watched the tea bags bobbing in the hot water. He tried to convince himself it was for the best to let her go.

As he set the timer to steep the tea bags, Earl tried to slow down his breathing. He tried to ignore the tears welling up in his eyes, tried to stop his hands from shaking. Tried to ignore the gurgling in his stomach.

The timer went off. The tea was ready.

With a tray across his lap, Earl got the two cups of tea into the living room. Jenny was still on the couch, looking through the printouts.

"Here." Earl set her cup on the coffee table. "I hope peppermint is okay."

She answered in an especially soft voice. "Thank you."

They sat and sipped their tea, Earl trying to ignore all the things roiling inside of him. After several minutes he set the cup down. "Fine."

"What?"

"I'll talk to her."

Jenny wouldn't let Earl go without getting cleaned up a bit first. On the way they stopped by the general store for breath mints.

When they got to Gloria's apartment, Earl and Jenny hovered around outside. Her place was bustling with activity. Apparently Gloria was in the process of moving right that minute. A couple of men pushed out carts loaded with boxes. From inside came the noise of more boxes moving around.

Jenny chuckled. "I guess we got here just in time."

"Um." Earl tugged at his collar—why was it so tight? "Maybe it's a sign."

"No. You are going to go in there and talk to her."

Earl put his hand on his chest. He breathed in deep then let it out. "Okay." He started to wheel forward then looked back at Jenny. "You're coming with me, right?"

"Nope." She patted him on the arm and winked. "You're on your own."

Earl took a deep breath and went in. He wheeled his way around the boxes at the door. "Hello?"

There was the murmuring of voices from the back room. Gloria and another woman came out. When Gloria saw Earl, she smiled uncertainly. "Well, hello there, Blue Eyes."

The second woman was carrying a box. She smiled at Earl and excused herself.

Earl sat there stupidly, staring at Gloria. She stared back. He coughed and gestured at the boxes around them. "I see you're about all packed up."

"Yes, yes."

Earl nodded. He tried to smile. She smiled back. He locked his fingers together. She folded her arms.

He rubbed the back of his neck. "So, I suppose you're all set to move away?"

"Um, yes. All set." She waved her arms. "My sons and their families are helping me."

"So I guess you know where you're going." He chuckled.

"Yes." She started to elaborate but stopped herself. Bit her lip.

They fell into silence again. Earl started bobbing his head, trying to shake the words out of his brain. Gloria leaned against the wall, her arms still folded.

Earl tried to make small talk. "So, it's odd—I only started to get to know my way around Candlewick, and it's closing down. Nobody seems to understand why the state would shut it down."

"I think part of the problem was a budget deficit."

"Even so, I wouldn't think—"

"Of several million dollars."

"Oh." Finally, something in Earl's head shook loose. "Gloria, I am so sorry about everything that happened." He started rubbing his eyes. "I could have gotten you arrested. I'm so embarrassed."

"Oh, darlin'. . ." Gloria pulled a chair close and took Earl's hand.

He gripped her hand tightly, putting his other hand on top. "I did such a terrible thing to you."

"Your young girlfriend told me all about how you helped me." She smiled. "She also said something about you confessing to protect me."

"It was all a mess."

Gloria squeezed Earl's hand. "I hear you were very brave."

"Stupid is more like it." But he smiled when he said it.

Gloria smiled back. She didn't say anything.

Earl grunted. "I've been by myself for so long, I forgot how to act around other people."

"You seemed okay to me."

"You're being too kind." Earl squeezed her hand again. "I thought I was better off alone. But I have learned these past few days that God created us to need Him. . .and to need other people."

"That's very profound."

"Well, someone told it to me." Earl started wringing his hands. "I was so worried about getting close to you that I blindly talked the county sheriff into thinking you were a killer." He rubbed the back of his neck again. "Of course, I never believed it."

"Didn't you?" She raised a playful eyebrow.

"Not really." He gave her a crooked smile. "But I was so busy pushing you away that it never occurred to me to trust you."

"Next time, you will."

"Next time?" Earl raised his eyebrows. "You get into this sort of trouble often?"

"Eh, only once in a while." She winked. "But not much."

A strange sound gurgled out of Earl. It took him a few seconds to realize it was his laughter. He had forgotten what it sounded like. He liked it.

She laughed with him. He liked the sound of that, too.

Earl wiped a tear from his eye. "I just hope you can forgive me."

"Of course, Blue Eyes." Gloria squeezed his knee. "Not that there's anything to forgive."

"You're very gracious." Earl waved a hand at the boxes around them. "So, can I help?"

"I think we've about got it. But you can supervise, if you like."

"It's what I do best." Earl locked his fingers together. "And can I get contact info to reach you at your new home?"

Gloria flashed him a knowing smile. She went to the table, grabbed a sealed envelope, and handed it to Earl. The envelope was addressed to him. He looked up with a quizzical look. She said, "It's my new address, phone number, and e-mail address. Your young lady friend said you might want that." She blushed. "That is, if you should happen to want to e-mail me sometime."

Earl grunted. "If I don't e-mail you, don't take it personally. But the rest of the information will come in handy." He smiled as he stuck the envelope in his shirt pocket. "I may even come visit."

"I hope you do."

He averted his eyes. "You know, I still love Barbara."

"I wouldn't expect you to stop. I still love my Dwight."

As Gloria returned to her moving, Earl kept to the side. Over the course of the next hour or so, he got a chance to meet Gloria's family. He watched the proceedings, chipping in with the occasional comment here and there.

Earl watched Gloria, coming to terms with his feelings for her. He was nervous about starting a new relationship, but he was excited.

After all, what's the worst that could happen?

CHRIS WELL has spent most of his adult life writing for and editing magazines, including Bill and Gloria Gaither's *Homecoming Magazine*, *Christian Bride*, and *Alfred Hitchcock's Mystery Magazine*. Also a novelist and a longtime fan of detective stories, Chris is thrilled to be writing his first series of cozy mysteries. He and his wife make their home in Tennessee, where he is hard at work on his next novel(s). Visit him online at www.StudioWell.com.

You may correspond with this author by writing:
Chris Well
Author Relations
PO Box 721
Uhrichsville, OH 44683

Look for more
Hometown Mysteries. . .
where love and suspense meet
at a bookstore near you!